I0760670

Jan Bitencourt

BETA VERSION

WeBook Publishing - English Edition

Published by WeBook Publishing – Los Angeles, CA

For information, please email info@webookpublishing.com

First English Edition

Hardcover

ISBN: 978-1-966892-10-6
LCCN: 2025917080
Written by Janine Bitencourt
Translator: Nathalia Coppa
Editor: Ana Silvani
Copy Editor: Maria Acero
Cover Design: Danilo Borges
Interior Formatting: WeBook Publishing

Manufactured in the United States of America

Note: Much care and technique were employed in editing this book. However, there can be no assurance that it will be free of minor typing errors, printing issues, or even conceptual ambivalence. In any such case, we ask that the issue be notified to our customer service at the e-mail address info@webookpublishing.com. Thank you!

BETA VERSION

To Lorenzo,
the boy who found the writer in me first.

To Elza,
in memoriam.

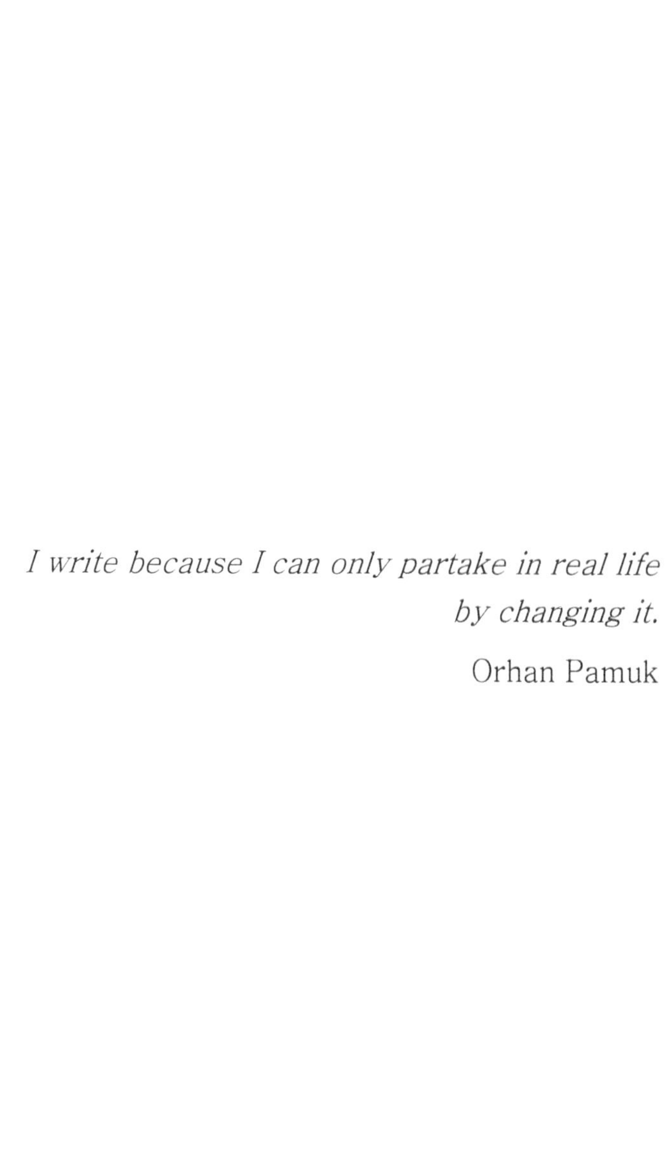

I write because I can only partake in real life by changing it.

Orhan Pamuk

Prologue

Thirteen years separate the Brazilian and American editions of this book. Back in 2012, I was still living in the countryside of São Paulo, tentatively exploring the path of writing, taking courses on crafting micro-stories and screenplays. The idea for this novel was born out of a writing course I took with a Brazilian publisher at the beginning of that year. Just three months later, it was finished and selected as the best among the participants.

I spent months editing it, asking for feedback from friends and my favorite authors, until finally, in December of that same year, it was launched at *Livraria da Vila.* The following year, I secured a bilingual Portuguese-German edition and traveled to Jena for a university reading to mark its release. That opportunity allowed me to move back to São Paulo, publish a second Brazilian edition, take more writing courses, and even start teaching short fiction in both in-person and online workshops. I also wrote a second book, but it ended up in a drawer.

Life took many turns, and twelve years later, I was granted a U.S. work visa with this award-winning novel as one of the key requirements. Since it was my only publication, many friends weren't even aware of its existence, and grew curious to read it. That's when I sent a copy to Ana Silvani at WeBook, and she agreed to translate and publish it in English.

Revisiting the book has been both gratifying and challenging. Is an author expected to improve the story and characters with their new references and years of experience? Is it worth updating the plot with current elements like AI? I'll admit that the temptation was real.

But my best friend once said: "The best thing about writing a book is getting rid of it." So, I chose the path of less suffering and focused only on reviewing sections or words that felt out of place or awkward after all these years. My son was 7 when the book first came out in Brazil and he's nearly 20 now. There are still some steamy scenes that I feel embarrassed about, imagining people I know reading, especially given the semi-autobiographical premise. Many of my parents' older friends were convinced everything I wrote actually happened to me in Madrid. And who could blame them? The whole idea behind the novel was exploring the boundary between reality and fiction.

Ultimately, this book brought me a lot of joy when I was 35, and I hope it continues to do so at 48, now in a language that may reach even more readers. And, who knows, maybe even a producer eager to help me realize my next dream: seeing it adapted for the big screen or TV.

Enjoy the read.

São Paulo – 2012

Once my bags had been checked, I tried to remember if there was anything else I might have forgotten to pack. I searched for my reflection in the hand mirror in my purse, and while looking around, I noticed I was the only redhead with unpainted nails and a makeup-free face in the VIP lounge at Guarulhos Airport. I tried to think, but my mind was jumbled. I had absolutely no expectations for my trip to Europe.

The piano player wrestled over the keys as the woman seated next to me mumbled nonsensical song lyrics. Everyone ate because the food was free, and a waitress ran around collecting and clearing the leftovers.

I sought distance from my routine to start a new novel. My editor had suggested Madrid since the new book had a travel guide angle, but lately, I'd felt lazy about certain adventures.

I wished I could send someone in my place. Perhaps an assistant, a doppelganger, a clone, maybe even a character. Suddenly, as if someone suggested from-me-to-me:

"What if you don't board the plane?"

I found the idea stupid, but it persisted.

"If you're only doing this to write a book, why fly so far away?"

The cold European air at this time of year was an excellent excuse. My favorite authors had walked through the cities, cafés, and subways of the Old World in search of inspiration, leaving behind memorable stories and books. But that was long ago.

"Everything you need can be found on the internet. How many millions of photos have been taken at all these places? The amount of information and tips that are available online is endless. It's easy to describe a city with some great references and a bit of imagination."

A small smile grew at the corner of my mouth as I realized this could be an incredible exercise. Maybe even more intense and rich than wandering around the city, picturing scenes and conversation, and returning home with a maxed-out credit card from all the clothes I didn't need.

"That's how you're supposed to write a book. Do you really think Dante went to hell?"

The thought felt convincing. Or perhaps I allowed it to be. The facts are easy to control when the author is responsible for creating everything and dictating each character's actions.

I've never been one of those writers who gained much out of a trip. A new destination meant an interruption in my lifestyle, making it difficult to get back into the swing of things when I returned home.

As I scrolled on my phone, I saw a picture of him playing guitar. His back was towards the camera as he sat by the fire on a beach in this picture taken by our daughter. I knew João wouldn't send me a "have a good trip" text, but those new lyrics were mine. Just mine, even though he'd never admit it.

Sinking deeper into the leather chair, I decided to start my trip then.

I established that Beta would be the name of the character who would travel in my place. I felt as though she had existed for some time and would know how to enjoy Madrid better than I ever could.

As I mentally listed the feelings that came with flying first class, I found a picture online of the airline's first-class dinner menu for that evening. I posted it on social media to my

15,000 followers as if I had taken it, already imagining myself accommodated in seat 2B.

I laughed as the comments wishing me a good trip flooded in. Things didn't need to be true for people to believe them.

I began to describe Beta in a more glamorous way, as autofiction allows me to: also divorced (and a writer with a past history that we shared), but child-free, fearless, and seductive in a way that will be kind of impossible for me to be. She wore black heeled boots and a *Ruby Woo Red* overcoat that hung just below the bend of her knees, which flared as she walked. Like in the "Sleeping Beauty and the Airplane" short story, I remembered the Gabriel Garcia Márquez words for Beta to be "a supernatural apparition that existed only for an instant, and disappeared into the crowd of the terminal".

The gate was quickly packed with phones, tablets, and frenetic laptops, along with their anxious owners. Using a pen to start writing on a blank sheet of paper made me feel like the oldest thing in the world. But things were looking up. I'd have ten days to convince myself that I flew to Madrid and found what I was looking for, whatever that may be.

Day one

Beta arrived in Madrid in one piece and decided to venture onto the subway to get to her hotel. As a made-up character, she didn't feel the pain of wearing heels for a long time, wandering almost weightlessly through the city streets, and her suitcase never bothered her as she took the subway, taking the line 8 to line 4, then line 1 to get to *Gran Via,* like walking through life in a well edited social media reel with background music.

Leaving the station without a strand of her long, Instagrammable blonde hair out of place, she found herself directly on *Calle de la Montera.* Her hotel was soon found next to the corner McDonald's, a modern building with halls decorated with old artwork. Beta accommodated herself in a room with a rooftop view that she deserved (instead of the boring room with absolutely no view I had chosen for myself just to write).

At the right time, far away from Spain, I would call home and ask the usual questions. There wouldn't be much to say, as I never gave anyone a reason to worry about.

Unlike Beta, I've been more human: gloomy and quite inconsistent, nothing like being picturesque. I didn't want to board the flight or return home. I canceled my ticket at the airline desk and requested that my bags be removed from the plane. "Mrs. Alberta Fable, your ticket has been canceled. How would you like to pay the fine?" I heard a shrill voice ask. I paid in cash and wasn't asked to explain the unexplainable. Grabbing a taxi, I made my way to the hotel closest to the airport. That's where I slept as Beta flew and where I would stay unless I changed my mind along the way (again).

My imagination took me to Madrid as the book began to walk alongside the character through the cold streets, beneath a cloudy sky, and among tall, dry trees with tourists from around the world. I typed *Calle de la Montera, Madrid, España* into the search bar, and in less than a second, Beta became a blue dot on my computer. From the intersection of *Montera* and *Gran Via*, you could easily spot the *Telefónica* Building, the Spanish capital's first skyscraper.

She put on her remarkable red coat and walked towards *Plaza Mayor*, guided by the smell of cinnamon and toasted cream wafting from the cafes serving churros and hot chocolate. Through the Christmas stands and living statues, she eventually found herself at the *Mercado de San Miguel,* packed with people snacking and drinking wine. Beta scanned every inch of the antiquated architecture, its various styles, and its neighbors. She wanted to taste everything the city had to offer.

If I had any limits, my character would easily surpass them. Beta believed in the power of chance and destiny, an ingenuity I never had. My common sense wouldn't influence her actions. She'd be incorrigibly optimistic, armed with a fierce will, and always believing the universe conspired in her favor.

She had forgotten how *guapo* the Europeans were and enjoyed the feeling of all eyes on her. During that winter, everything seemed more vibrant and alive, people were really looking for genuine connections. She absorbed the city with a childlike wonder. She wondered if the men would think she was only smiling for them, but truthfully, she was flirting with everyone, a magnetic presence that was hard to ignore.

The trip had already been worth it. Despite its sharpness, the air was truly inspiring. When she caught her reflection, it stared back with a look of renewal. There she stood, with her hands in her pockets, her neck shrunken into a turtleneck, and a freedom she gained from being a woman without a care in the world. She wandered about without a map or phone, and spoke perfect Spanish (which I've never achieved), pretending to be a local, and even enjoyed tapas among smoking men, as the Spanish often did during their lunch breaks.

After returning to her room, she messaged her good friend Anita, who lived in the city, to let her know she had arrived. At this point, she craved being with familiar people to share her first impressions of the city. Her friend recommended a quick lunch at the always-crowded *Mercado de San Miguel* the following day.

Before her first *siesta* in the city, she took a long shower with the name Miguel lingering in the back of her mind, despite her enjoyment of this long-awaited trip. Perhaps her presence there wasn't accidental. After all, a person named Miguel played a role in her marriage ending.

Two years ago. Guarulhos International Airport - GRU.

Beta was just another blonde in a scarf with red nails and light makeup in line boarding a flight to Paris. She was miserable, lost, and destroyed. The news of her husband's affair was recent, so she struggled to digest the truth.

Her childhood friend Anita had been living in Paris, and she decided to go to her for a shoulder to cry on. She needed to clear her head and try to understand the situation from a different perspective.

The airline clerk's mouth moved in slow motion: "Do you have another valid passport?" She smiled, not understanding the joke, and asked, "Why?" before looking down at her photo, taken at least six years ago, on the passport that had expired precisely twenty days ago. She believed in God, but there, she was sure that Murphy's law was calling the shots.

Stunned, she got out of line and canceled her ticket, but she refused to return home and instead bought a last-minute ticket and headed toward *Morro de São Paulo* in Bahia State, despite not having packed a swimsuit or any other suitable clothing to face the Bahian summer.

It was an incredible week: she cried, drank, surrendered, and slowly took back the reins of her life. The euros she had packed were used on a haircut and clothing she bought at stores owned by foreigners who had become locals. She practiced yoga, made new friends, and wrote feverishly. She wrote while she was drunk, sober, hungover, crying, in the morning, at dawn, standing up, lying down, as if nothing else mattered in this life. As if it would save her. As if that story genuinely wanted to exist.

To return with a concrete decision about her long and deteriorating relationship, she went to a local *forró* party on her last night. There she drank *caipirinha* made with alcohol that was too sweet and went out that night with a man she had just met, enchanted by her without hearing a single word of her tragic story.

His name was Miguelangelo, and he lived in Madrid.

It was a great night without much conversation, just an intense and real connection that proved she wasn't dead. Miguelangelo left forever, and she lived happily for a few moments.

As soon as she returned, she watched her marriage go up in smoke. Her husband couldn't take the retribution, but her family was relieved to see her back. They always sensed that one day they'd lose her to her etherealness.

Two new nicknames emerged from this experience: "separated" and "writer." The pain was transformed into a sharp novel. Her book garnered excellent repercussions, resulting in a significant amount of work for her: a column at a respected magazine and an order for a new book.

The thought brought her back to the vapor-filled shower in Madrid.

Beta put on warm clothes as the sun had gone down in Spain.

She soon discovered she was in a gay neighborhood and walked the streets alone behind stylish and good-smelling men. She circled a few blocks, smoked a few cigarettes, and heard about a small club called *Why Not?*, which she found very suggestive.

A friend called to talk about her ex-husband. She pretended not to mind but forgot the path she was supposed to take. She stumbled upon a charming and warm pub called *La*

Casita. The bartender was Cuban, and the cook was Brazilian. There, she made some new friends: two Americans and a Canadian, with whom she sipped mojitos and enjoyed tapas.

They spoke English, carrying the joy and ingenuity of being in their twenties. All were very drunk and talked about futilities, new technology, and vacations.

Who was she again? And Beta told them to guess. Based on her English and physical appearance, they guessed various European nationalities but were surprised when she revealed her Brazilian heritage. She was very different from the stereotypical charming, shapely brunette.

They joked about inventing a new origin for her better suited for her paleness, which didn't align with the Brazilian summer. From then on, her origins changed: she now came from Transylvania, which was only one of the places where she maintained residence. They assigned her a new language and an age seven years younger, and she began to indulge in the chaos.

Beta laughed and imagined the incredible stories she could collect with a false identity. If she could have any superpower, she'd wish to switch bodies with other people so that she could feel a bit strange and new, like seeing the world through another window. She wouldn't mind if the experience were temporary because, all in all, she also liked being herself.

At a certain point in the night, the time when a conversation devolves into a sexual topic, she had to teach her new friends the Portuguese translation of whiskey dick, and they loved learning the new term *meia-bomba.*

Eventually, she felt tiredness and numbness in her legs. Travelling can be a bit tiring.

She smoked her last cigarette with Cecília, the Brazilian cook with a Spanish accent who had lived there for eight years and was married to an Englishman she met on the internet. She was surprised to hear that Beta traveled alone and encouraged her not to worry as her partner would arrive soon.

"I have an incredible capacity to attract confused men and overly romantic women," Beta thought as she walked the six blocks back to her hotel.

Day two

In São Paulo, I slept for twelve hours straight.

I was awakened by my daughter calling about some basic domestic issues and by the hotel housekeepers, who I asked to drop off the towels and return tomorrow to clean the rest of the room. I can't stand staying in this hotel room any longer. Thankfully, I had barely unpacked my bags.

As I had predicted, Julia was doing great. She was made for the world and seemed to adapt to it well. She looks a lot like me, a fact she hates while she strives to hide her freckles and dye her hair a horrendous vampy black. Her temperament, musical talents, and knack for numbers were inherited from her father. She has a fixation on technology and was my savior in moments of panic.

João was kind and present. It was funny how he gave our daughter all the care and attention he no longer gave me since the separation. When do couples unlearn how to live together? At this point, he wouldn't ask Julia about me like before. Such emotional topics always take me back to one thing: cigarettes.

In Madrid, Beta went outside to the hotel entrance to smoke.

Had she been there long enough to notice the prostitutes who lurked in the area? According to the online reviews, her hotel was well known to be in a corner of prostitution in Madrid.

In São Paulo, it was time to switch hotels because hotels around big airports are not the most inspiring places in the world. I asked the taxi driver to leave me in *Baixo Augusta,* and I'd figure it out from there.

Then I checked in at a place near a presumed prostitution spot. Either here in São Paulo or in Madrid, this story needed real-life elements to be coherent. "What are the odds of getting hit on while smoking at the entrance of the hotel?" I noticed that my improvised summer outfit (because of my winter luggage) was a light silk nightdress, and maybe the sex worker was expecting me to pay to use her spot for leisure. Well, I don't know exactly what happened, but I almost swallowed the cigarette out of embarrassment.

Redheaded competition? The prostitutes may have wondered. Or was it just a joke from an unsuspecting onlooker? Would Beta be up for it? I suppressed the urge to write a more audacious chapter for my character.

Beta decided to go to the *Prado.*

Without looking down, she walked through the streets and was struck by the beauty of the buildings around her. The *Art Nouveau* mosaics, a blend of Parisian and Oriental influences, and the beautiful iron balconies with stone carvings all vied for her attention. It was like walking through a masterclass in architecture.

Eventually, she reached the *Paseo del Prado*, guided by the yellow lights that illuminated the wide streets. Around her, dry leaves danced with the cold winds as she approached the museum.

As if jolted awake, she snapped out of her trance and found herself in front of a white marble statue that read:

La Magdalena Penitente - Antonio Canova

A sensual and semi-nude Mary Magdalene, kneeling on a stone, weeps for her sinful past and meditates beside a skull. This is a supreme example of Canova's artistic skill and imagination.

It was difficult for Beta to describe the feeling art evoked within her. She tried to explain to her parents, who didn't raise her on books, music, art, or cinema, the visceral reaction she felt from a piece of classic work.

Her Sunday morning in Madrid was dedicated to contemplating this kneeling Mary Magdalene, perfectly sculpted on a single block of white marble with infinite details. She observed the wisps of hair on her forehead, eyes lowered, tears rolling down her cheeks, and shoulders hunched from carrying the weight of the world. Who knows what she was waiting for as she sat there with her hands lying on her knees, wholly surrendered.

The energy of that piece hypnotized Beta. The large bench beside the statue proved useful as she sat there and wept beneath her sunglasses for quite some time. It couldn't fit into a picture, as it won't fit here in the words Beta wished to speak. She wanted to take it home, but figured it was a bit too heavy, in every sense of the word.

If Beta lived here, she might visit every day, always bringing something that resembles what Mary Magdalene seems to be asking for: perhaps some recognition or devotion, maybe an identification with her pain, exhaustion, and surrender. Or even just the salvation of her purity and levity. All the while, that skull sits beside her, laughing at the ridiculousness of humanity.

Beta became static. She deeply wished for Mary Magdalene to suddenly come alive, like the living statues that populated the streets of Madrid, and go to a café with her.

She would tell incredible stories and share entrancing truths, packed with irony, while revealing her vulnerable side and remarkable strength. All through a fascinatingly melancholic gaze. Had she been truly a whore or the companion to a wonderful man? She'd tell Beta her secrets.

After all, what is real? If this sculpture isn't, she doesn't know what else would be.

She's ancient, yet she translates a frightening modern agony. You can see the helplessness, absence, impotence, and solitude. Her dress falls from her body, but nothing matters more than her submission to the path she chose that guides her to wherever it wants.

Almost an hour later, Beta recomposed herself.

"It's so pathetic to cry at the Prado," she thought. "Good thing Anita is late and I'm alone".

I don't know how I thought I could keep up the Madrid lie for over two days before slipping up. During my second day "traveling," an unknown number called. I answered before I could regret it. It was my editor.

"Al? Hi. It's me."

"New number, Carlos?"

"I got it yesterday. I didn't think you'd answer me."

"I answered by accident."

"I love you too, Alberta. How's Madrid?"

"Freezing, as predicted."

"And how's the book coming along?"

"Did you call to pressure me?"

"I've noticed your mood gets worse in the cold, huh?"

Four seconds of awkward silence. I love using those in moments like this instead of responding.

"Well, I called to remind you that Angelo asked you to meet him for lunch to discuss the translation and launch of your book in Spain. He called your hotel and didn't find you."

"The Spanish editor? I completely forgot, Carlos…"

I knew Angelo through his writing proposal to translate and publish my first book in Spain.

"I gave him your number, ok? He'll call you today."

"I hate these types of lunches. Could we do it online?"

"You're already there anyway, Al."

There was no point in arguing with Carlos. I agreed and quickly hung up, trying to think of a plan to avoid that meeting, weighing the different options to see how likely I could keep up my ruse.

Option 1: The Victim. All I'd need is a kind email pretending to have gotten a sudden case of viral pink eye. Any human contact must be avoided for at least five days.

Option 2: The Busy Bee. I could say I went to the publisher's office and didn't find him, but unfortunately, I would be traveling to inland Spain to conduct some book research and wouldn't be available.

Option 3: The Rude One. I'd admit that I didn't want to meet in person if it could be discussed virtually.

Option 4: The Freak. I'd throw my phone, which wouldn't stop ringing, at the wall and become unreachable from here on out.

"Hello."

"*Hola.* Alberta?"

"Yes. Angelo?"

"I've been trying to reach you since yesterday. Is it always this difficult?"

I tried to choose an excuse, but his thunderous voice derailed my train of thought.

"*Soy imposible…*" instantly regretting my poor Spanish attempt.

"I would love to meet up with you. Does today at 8 work?"

"No, no, I have plans with…"

"Tomorrow at 1 p.m., and I won't take no for an answer."

"Tomorrow? It's just that…"

"I have to go. I'll pick you up at your hotel. See you then."

I stood there, mad as hell that I couldn't control the situation. I took a deep breath and decided to send an email declining the invitation because of my viral pink eye. And then I'd send one to Carlos, swearing at him for putting me in this situation.

With that being said, it would be wise to call the Madrid hotel and let them know I switched hotels in case someone came looking for me. Okay… everything was now under control. It's time to take care of my character in Madrid. It reminded me of a time when having a virtual pet was a trend. Beta was my *Tamagotchi,* and I needed to feed her.

Beta remains in the Prado, wanting to be considered a piece of art or at least someone's muse, perhaps even the lover of a famous painter. She was too much for herself only, and couldn't wait to become the object of adoration in the life of a powerful man.

She was almost late to lunch with Anita after the meetup had been switched to the museum's cafeteria. It was an incredible space packed with modern people. Her friend seems thinner and taller than she remembered, tanned even in the winter, and a typical Brazilian type with the most beautiful chocolate skin and a contagious smile. After having added many other professions to her CV, Anita was now a stylist, stating, "I have a fluid career like the new generation." She was easy-to-like, always single but never alone, often changing men as if "they were clothes." After living there for many years, Anita was familiar with the coolest spots.

They drank more wine than at a typical lunch meet-up, so they decided to walk through the museum while they recovered from their alcohol-induced daze. Their laughter was loud enough to draw reprimanding looks from the security guards and curious glances from everyone else. What had been so funny?

For hours, they ambled about in front of the paintings, asking themselves how much each piece might cost while planning intricate heists to steal their favorite ones while standing much closer to the brushstrokes than permitted. They detested Gothic art, as they pretended to be witches. In the Renaissance section, they imagined the suffering those white and chubby bodies would experience today. Nothing compares to a girls' date, tipsy enough not to care about their behavior.

Anita had to leave, but they planned on seeing Juan Zelada later that night at *Sala El Sol*, a spot near Beta's hotel. Beta took the opportunity to ask Anita to bring one of her Spanish friends as a gift. Anita agreed that it was time for her to immerse herself in the native tongue fully. Their laughs echoed around the museum room.

Anita looked through her Facebook list for friends available to hang out, and Beta's interest gravitated to one of the four Miguels mentioned.

"I didn't know it was such a common name here."

"You didn't? It's like the name *Zé* in Brazil."

She texted the one Beta chose, inviting him to the concert that night. They said their goodbyes and agreed to meet up at Beta's hotel later that night near the prostitutes in the white long leather boots. They knew the *Prado* regulars had never experienced such a scandalous encounter as they had that afternoon.

Traveling alone felt strange. Maybe that's why I didn't board the plane.

They say women say an average of twenty thousand words a day. I have friends who would undoubtedly double that number if they were being interviewed. The fact of the matter is that by travelling alone, you spare useless comments and thoughts, the kind that only leave your mouth because silence is more uncomfortable when you're with someone.

Having dinner alone is uncomfortable. But it's also a lot tastier. The clarity of your thoughts isn't interrupted by your grocery list, your housekeeper's bonus, or your daughter's tight shoes. What a shame that I was never pleased by the menu.

At a table for two, I kept imagining who I'd pick to sit in the empty seat before me, and nobody really came to mind.

I looked at my phone between bites and noticed that people had become statistics. When my book was launched, I remembered how the readers started following me on Twitter, liking my Facebook page, and visiting my blog. I made it a point to know who each new fan was and almost thanked them for liking something of mine. When they were a celebrity, I would get insomnia.

Things changed when I was interviewed on TV. In the first hour, I gained 1,180 new followers, which ruined my retribution and symbolic acknowledgement plan.

From then on, what mattered were the numbers: 300 copies sold that week, 700 daily views on the blog, 15,000 Twitter followers who shared anything I wrote, 30 emails to respond to every day, and 600 friends waiting to be accepted on Facebook. Notifications would go off every minute on my phone, making the battery last only a few hours, while launch events for writer friends I *had* to attend under contract blended with virtual interviews, press releases, roundtables, bookstore events, and autographs. It became nothing more than a giant circus for the author to milk their masterpiece.

We learn to speak under the aura of an important person, directly to "my followers." Becoming a character of oneself while almost speaking in a condescending and arrogant third person. I don't know any author who hasn't grown tired of talking about their book. You become a salesperson, a publicist, and downright unbearable. And when you think about inviting someone for dinner, none of the 15,000 followers sounds palatable. Were they actually real or just avatars the editors created to feed the writers' egos? The virtual world is exhausting.

I received an empty email from Angelo. Even after clearing out my inbox, the email still came in empty. It wasn't a good time for technology to betray me.

Since I had to cancel my professional lunch with Angelo in real life, Beta deserved a fun fictional meeting in my place, without the weight of my "popularity." I imagined her choosing an older Spanish Miguel, not much older than us, handsome, intellectual, with a melancholic air.

In Spain, Beta quickly showered and dressed casually, promising not to drink anymore today. After the forties, the effects of the lunchtime wine took too long to pass, even for a fictional character. The hotel's concierge confirmed that *El Sol* was less than a mile away. She was early and decided to make her way over.

Time was typically an issue with her. She oscillated between being incredibly early and stressed by her tardiness.

Anita arrived arm in arm with Miguel (better in person compared to his Facebook picture), who, upon seeing Beta's smile, stopped abruptly and bowed theatrically. Beta greeted her new friend as he offered his other arm to escort her inside. Their laughter rang through with an almost instant intimacy, but Beta noticed his attempt to place his wedding ring in his pocket discreetly.

The music was good and encompassed a diverse, well-mixed blend of genres, including pop, soul, blues, and folk. Juan Zelada was Spanish but was incredibly popular in England, where he had just returned from with his band. The room was packed, and Miguel took the opportunity to hug Beta from behind while a slower song played. She whispered in his ear:

"You have no shame, huh?"

"Nope," he responded, smiling.

"I prefer it that way," Beta confessed.

"You look like you do."

"Hey, was that a compliment?"

"I adore courageous women."

"Like your wife, for example?" she decided to test him.

"That one doesn't even dare to leave her player husband."

"Hahahahaha. And why would she leave?"

"Because he's enchanted by his new Brazilian friend."

"*¡Soy yo!*"

"*Sí, sí.* And because he won't settle until he sleeps with her."

"Wow! Straight to the point?"

"I know you want it too."

"Really? Writers can be quite deceitful."

"Hmm, so let me read between the lines…"

"Hahaha. These metaphors are getting dangerous."

"I'm gonna get us some drinks. Stay exactly where you are."

Beta remembered she'd promised herself not to drink anymore, but she knew that she had never kept her promises. She just couldn't say no to Miguel.

It's challenging to sequence the following series of events as they all blurred together. The conversation was enhanced by the music, warmed by the ambiance, and elevated by the drinks. Altogether, it was incredible, but it lasted such a short time. The concert ended at midnight, and the crowd shuffled into other clubs. Anita had already disappeared with another friend.

Miguel walked Beta back to her hotel. He insisted on coming up, but Beta decided another day would be for the best. It was difficult to separate these two, and the man seems to have a thousand hands on her body. The more she mentioned she should go rest, the more he intensified his approach, attempting to persuade her to give in to his pleas. Their kiss left the prostitutes excited to the point where some wanted to join in. "Dangerous man. Too charming," Beta made a mental note. Miguel begged to see her again the next day. Beta answered with a mysterious smile. She liked setting fires and running away.

I saved the new chapter and lit a cigarette on my São Paulo hotel balcony.

Truthfully, I don't know why I gave my character to a married man as a love interest. Sometimes, the story just writes itself. Sometimes, it's the need to break your own rules. Not getting involved with committed men has always been my golden rule.

But Beta was just a character. Let the game continue.

Day three

I woke up invisible. It was as if the secret camera that we believe follows us 24/7 had been turned off. Instead of relief, there was emptiness. Contrary to what I'd imagined, the feeling of knowing I can be whatever I want to, without playing any role, filled me with anxiety.

After complaining so much about the overexposure I had recently endured, I found myself on the opposite side of the virtual world. My phone had no notifications, inboxes were empty, and no one needed me. Boredom crept up and smiled at me with its yellow teeth.

I restarted my laptop and phone to see if it had been a technical issue, as I have limited understanding of technology. I thought of Julia, my beautiful and geeky pre-teen. She'd be able to tell me what was happening. Perhaps a virus, a pending update, or an expired password?

Fuck! I'm over here hiding and can't call anyone. There weren't any appointments or birthdays I had to remember, right? Hmm. Today was João's day to pick up Julia from school. I wish I could be a fly on the wall to spy on their lunch. "Don't even think about it," I told myself, but I already had.

Before I knew it, I was dressed and calling a taxi. The taxi driver probably thought it was a robbery attempt with a scarf wrapped around my head and giant sunglasses to obscure my features, but I just didn't want to be recognized.

The weather in São Paulo was expected to bring a downpour during rush hour. The taxi's air conditioner couldn't hide the fact that it was dry, polluted, and 89°. I planned on lurking behind the window. All I wanted was to keep an eye on them.

João arrived on his motorcycle. I felt proud to have chosen him as my daughter's father. He was over 40 and as charming as ever. He wasn't one of those dads whose teenagers asked them to wait at the corner. You could see it on Julia's face.

She waited at the door with her friends while he parked. The moment didn't last long, but it happened in slow motion for me. There stood the two most important people in my life, who looked so alike it hurt.

Her friends were delighted when they saw João. He always took a picture with one of them before leaving, without any annoyance or discomfort. He was very loving towards her, which was noticeable as he put her helmet on with a smile. Why didn't we stay together? This was our daughter's eternal question.

I tried using a metaphor to explain, but I knew I probably wouldn't be able to. I considered using a soccer example, but gave up because the sport wasn't a shared passion between us. At the time of the separation, I recall telling her that our marriage was like the sandcastles we built by the ocean. It looked beautiful, tall, and strong, until the tide rose and a wave came and washed everything away.

Reconstruction requires time and specific circumstances. But the sand took too long to dry, and the sun burned our backs. We were hungry, and we both ran away in search of crumbs, abandoning the castle's reconstruction.

The first time I told this story, it was a disaster. My daughter's strong critical reasoning didn't approve of my spur-of-the-moment excuse. "What about me?" She'd ask in disbelief, "Was it not worth it to focus on the castle for me?"

I didn't respond at that moment. In my head, I planned to distract her with the sound of the ice cream truck, the cute boys on the beach, or a ride on the banana boat. My mistake. It's better to save money on ice cream now for the future therapy bills.

To this day, she doesn't accept any of his little 'girlfriends'. Girls who are groupies and about 15 years younger than him. She always tells me he's doing it to provoke me, and I let her believe what she wants to.

What do I think of all this? I think I miss something about it, but I don't know what. I'm also curious how he survives without someone as cool as me. Cool, modest, and ironic.

João disappeared down the street with Julia on his back, and I felt a mix of emotions: happy yet sad, resigned yet melancholic, nostalgic yet practical. It just wasn't meant to be. Letting go was a difficult lesson for me, followed by the lesson on letting go of the control I believed I had on everything.

I asked the taxi driver to turn back and drop me off at the hotel.

They'd survive without me. I'd learn to do without them.

When I arrived at the hotel, I saw a missed call on my phone. Has technology finally started working again? I returned the call from Spain.

The hotel concierge said I'd received flowers from a man who wanted to stay anonymous. He'd also left a card. I assumed it was from Angelo wanting to reschedule our lunch. But why flowers? Did he search for me at the hotel?

The concierge wanted to know who he should deliver the flowers to, as he didn't find me. "How could we meet up if I weren't in Madrid? Did I forget to cancel the reservation?" I couldn't remember. Curiously, I claimed I wasn't in the city and needed to know what was written on the card urgently. He started to read it back to me:

"*... and the female, laughing, denied what I begged for. What should be given and more than given, eaten. Then, the lady killed me...*" *Hago de las palabras de Drummond las mías, loco para decirte el resto en tu oído hoy, en mi cama. Tu ...*

"Perdona señora, pero no reconozco la firma," the poor man said lightly.

I almost died of embarrassment. The concierge was getting uncomfortable as the end of the note approached. "*Por Dios,* who had sent me that?" I don't remember whether I hung up on the poor man or said goodbye to him. I just know I seemed catatonic. It must've been a mistake.

Would it be best to call Angelo? I decided against it. I'd send a formal email agreeing to the book translation details and what he and Carlos had planned for the launch.

"Yes, focus on your work, Alberta." Those flowers are not mine. That erotic poem was taken from a book that Drummond only allowed to be published once he was dead. I went to Google to find the title: "The Girl Reveals a Thigh." It sounded quite audacious. Some lucky woman awoke a strong instinct within someone and would have an excellent time that night. A Brazilian poet on top of that?

If it couldn't be for me, it would have to be for Beta. This was the perfect segue to give my character a more *caliente* chapter. Enough joking around. I'm gonna light this book on fire, out of rage.

Beta slammed the bathroom door in the world's face. She had decided to sleep with Miguel.

Smiling like a child up to no good, she reached the shower. The running water played like a soundtrack as the water drops fell on the bathroom tiles, echoing throughout the walls. A humid scent filled the air as her vision blurred and her pores cleared.

Yesterday whirled down the drain and slid away. Beta exfoliated her dead skin roughly, so harshly in fact, her new skin turned pink and red from the abrasive scrubbing. She shut the cold faucet gradually, letting the temperature build until only scorching water could be felt. Strands of water burned red paths down her body, leaving behind goosebumps from a mixture of pleasure and pain.

She wrote in the air, hummed a lullaby, danced with herself, and daydreamed. Finding the cold wall, she stamped her back on the tile. Her tardiness soon broke down the door and carried her into the world. Dripping a trail of water on the floor, as if her hair was protesting to stay longer in the shower. "Damn internal timing. Late again!" she swore once she noticed the time.

Miguel was already waiting at the hotel entrance. She wanted "to see his books", a dumb and impulsive excuse to get invited to his apartment. He had left his family and business in Barcelona, as if creating a divide of reality and pleasure. She didn't fully understand what he did or why, but she also wouldn't feel guilty about going out with someone who is married. Life is short, right?

It was an impressive apartment. Everything in it was strategically arranged for the conquest fueled by desire: indirect lighting that created a sensual mood, smooth music emanating from expensive speakers at the perfect volume to be felt down to the bone, and minimalist yet intentional decor meant not to distract from the actual point of entertainment. His library was designed to impress and was packed with wonderful Spanish authors. And the cherry on top: a view of the *Plaza de las Cibeles* invaded the apartment through the living room's floor-to-ceiling windows.

Miguel smelled good and distanced himself with the typical European timidity. He didn't even look like the guy who had ravished her at the hotel entrance the night before. She noticed he'd opened two buttons on his shirt as he brought over a bottle of wine, maybe to cool down his own heat.

His eyes never left Beta as he spoke in a low and deep tone. It was best not to think about how many women had sat on the same exact sofa she was sitting on now.

"Tienes hambre?" Miguel asked as he offered her a glass of wine. Beta simply shook her head with a lingering smile on her lips. He took it as a compliment, without irony. Better that

way. She wouldn't be able to maintain that superiority for much longer.

She desired this man. Dreamt about him all night long. She planned on not sleeping alone. In fact, she planned on not sleeping at all.

Miguel wanted to know if she had received the flowers. Beta responded that they must've been delivered to the wrong address. He laughed and mentioned that it didn't matter. Unlike her, he preferred to speak rather than write. But confessed that a good book always came in handy in times like this.

"Choose one, and I'll whisper it to you," his thunderous voice asked.

"I want a…steamier one. What do you recommend?" She encouraged him with a coy seduction.

"*Ahora?*" He asked, placing his glass on the table, when he saw that Beta was being serious.

Slowly, he sat beside her with "Natural Love," a book of collected erotic poems by Carlos Drummond de Andrade. Open to a marked page, it was clear it was already memorized, given the worn state of the pages. The heat from his body could be felt intensely as the distance between them decreased, with each word of the poem slowly whispered in Beta's ears, lingering on her like the touch of his hands from the other night.

"The tongue licks the red petals of the unfurled rose…"

He slowly lifted her dress with one hand as if it had experienced every woman in the world and wasn't intimidated by any of them. His thunderous tone transformed Spanish into another language, absorbing Beta, tantalizing all the senses as it vibrated through her.

"The tongue toils a certain hidden button…"

In one swift and precise motion, he pulled Beta onto his lap and dropped the book. She lost all remnants of superiority and the illusion of control. He was ready to fuck. So was she.

"...and weaves delightful variations of gentle rhythms."

His words were broken by the movements of his tongue on her neck, and their breathing increased in pace as the excitement grew. His voice was as hard as his cock, slowly slipping into Beta. She felt all of Miguel inside her. His warm breath brushed up against her, tickling trails to her heat, and his voice melted her entirely as his hands pulled a fistful of her hair while he consumed her.

"And lick, lavish, laud the haired lycorine grotto."

He flipped her onto all fours toward the windows and continued. Each time more firmly, more roughly, and more painfully. Beta moaned loudly as if she were notifying all the tiny people walking by the fountain in the square. She wanted to be seen there with Miguel.

The pleasure came quickly as they hungrily bit each other, words broken by grunts and moans, never did the words stop. And the rest, no matter how good a narrator I was, would be impossible to translate out of context.

Nightfall encompassed São Paulo, and I could no longer focus on the book.

I had a long day, and looking at the *Augusta* Avenue packed with people enjoying summer at the bars, I remembered a little alternative club around there that I'd love to visit. At the door, I cut the line, staring down the hostess with the confidence of someone who is a *habitué*, even though I've never set foot in such a place. But it worked, I was in.

The drinks were nothing special, but the music was great for dancing. Four vodkas were needed to repel the heat. I rambled on with the music, and before I knew it, I was locked in a sizzling kiss with a man just like the others. Then with another. Or was it the same one? All so alike and blurred together. I couldn't hear what they said. Not anymore. Because of the music and the repetition.

Going beyond that wasn't worth it today. I didn't want anyone in my cave. I laughed out loud when I noticed the pun. The world was spinning, signaling it was time to go home. I instinctively searched for my phone to check the time, then remembered I had left it at the hotel. I needed to disconnect a bit. My story was moving too fast.

The sound of my hollow heels echoed on the sidewalk. I walked four blocks watching the lights, traffic, and nightlife of the city I adore more than any other in the world. At least, I didn't have to drive home drunk. My hiding place is delightful. I'm on vacation from life, social masks, waxing, and friends that demand electrifying news. I was free from the scale, the housekeeper, the grocery store, the gardener, dad, and mom.

I dismantled my outfit into pieces around the room and turned everything off.

I've traveled too much today. Living can also be a bit tiring.

Beta's version

I had slammed the bathroom door in the world's face when I decided to sleep with Miguel.

He was already at the hotel entrance once again. I let him wait a bit longer, giving him time to stew. My lust needed to be controlled, and he needed to be left alone with his fantasies. I knew he'd arrive excited. Very excited. Yesterday, I gave him some ideas about what he could expect from me if we were to see each other again.

"*Vente conmigo, que te voy a llevar al delir,*" he promised.

We were going to his apartment in Madrid. Before meeting him downstairs, I decided to take off my panties. If we stopped somewhere before, my dress wouldn't hide anything. But I knew we'd get straight to the point as fast as his car could go.

He knew how to play but had found a worthy competitor in me.

The route was short, and the wind was cold. Yet it wasn't capable of lowering the degree of sexual tension in that car; the heat was unbearable. I felt his gaze on my thighs and moved my dress slightly, leaving no doubt that everything would be as quick and easy as he'd like.

At each red light, he'd pull me close and bite me gently, whispering "*Qué ganas que te tengo, gamberra.*" The dizziness that hit me was like I'd taken two shots of pure alcohol, and it went straight to my senses.

I hope there isn't a camera in his building's elevator. Neither of us seemed to mind. Suddenly, there were only the two of us in the world, in the elevator, and in the mirror. Never has a winter seemed so hot like during the time it took us to ride the elevator up to his penthouse.

We entered his apartment, and I figured it would be wise to cool down the excitement. I asked for a glass of wine and took longer than usual to recompose myself in the bathroom. Let the game begin, I started to enjoy it.

I had strolled through the *Plaza de las Cibeles* earlier that day, but my best memories were yet to come. From his penthouse, we could see its lights inciting all the fantasies through the living room's large windows.

He promised he'd behave himself if I maintained a safe distance, all while bringing over some wine and undoing two buttons on his shirt, once again in an effort of releasing his own heat. His eyes were cemented on me as he spoke.

Grabbing my glass, I walked towards the bookshelf and chose a book higher than my five-inch heels could reach. My dress slid up, revealing my bare skin, a retribution for the open shirt. He came over to toast with a bit more ferocity than expected. Et voilá!

"*Quiero tus besos. Quiero sentirme tan adentro de ti y tan profundo,*" he said while conquering me, inch by inch.

I reached for a random book, which I intentionally let fall out of my hand. He knew what I wanted. Kneeling in front of me, he lifted what little I had of my dress and pressed my body against the shelf while he sucked on me.

"*Ah, como te siento.*"

He laid me down on the sofa and while he sucked me with perfect pressure, at a slow pace so as not to rush my climax, his pants perfectly revealed the size and contour of what he had in store for me and that had already excited me so much the night before when we almost had sex standing up on the street in front of my hotel.

Drunk with lust, it was my turn to reciprocate and see if his cock worked even better than his mouth. I received Miguel hard, so wet that my orgasm came easily and intensely, almost violently, but just right to make him cum all over me, laughing, sweaty, receiving his kisses and licks, as if our climax wasn't enough to cool things down. We both wanted more, like unsatisfied sex beasts.

We devoured each other on the floor, then on the other couches, later in the shower, then standing up, marking the windows with two hot bodies. Miguel fucked up my senses with words whispered closely to my ears, teaching me a non-poetic Spanish.

There I was, personifying all women in the world, finally free from the shackles of judgment to be their naughtiest selves when they surrendered to the moment and to a man who knows how to give pleasure. With each climax, the others' desire ignited and restarted the caresses, the fiery kisses, new positions, more wine, and scratches, in a night that'd make Alberta blush.

At 4 a.m., I decided I'd go back to my hotel. He protested, not wanting the night to end. Neither of us would give up. We were tired and happy. Miguel took me home, promising many more nights like that one.

I can't believe Alberta had doubts about coming to this beautiful and crazy city.

She needed to breathe in new air. Opening up her Facebook, I decided it was time to interfere. I chose a sentence that summed up my night. After all, I had found the best teacher in the city to learn Spanish with, I laughingly thought to myself, and posted:

"I never liked Spanish, but it sounds heavenly when whispered."

Genius! I'm a genius!

Day four

Alberta awoke but couldn't open her eyes.

An immense hangover made her wonder if she had drunk spiked vodka. She felt it all: a headache, a sore throat, and body aches. She searched for cold medication and took two doses. She later regretted it as her body couldn't stand allopathy. What if it got worse, and she actually put herself under the weather because of the medicine?

Checking the time on her phone, she found many notifications from people commenting on her late-night Facebook post.

"Damn, did I drunkenly post something stupid?" She grimaced, already predicting disaster ahead.

She almost fell back when she read what was posted on her page at 4:45 a.m. "I never liked Spanish, but it sounds heavenly when whispered." The sentence flashed at her like a neon sign.

"It's not possible… Beyond schizophrenia, I now have Alzheimer's, too?" Alberta thought.

Everyone wanted to know who the new hottie was. They requested more photos and made sarcastic comments. She decided to play along, saying that a picture of her new "fling" would be posted soon.

In the shower, the aches and pains persisted. Potentially grew with the recently added worry. She tried to rid herself of the cigarette smell that clung to her body, even after scrubbing herself with the hotel's soap. "It really is just hotel soap. What did I expect?"

After wiping down a spot on the mirror, she saw a raccoon staring back: smudged eyes, an extreme paleness, blunt hair, and dry skin. She chugged all the bottles of sparkling water from the minibar and decided it was best to go back to sleep.

Before she went back to rest, she opened her book to jot down some ideas and felt a strange sensation for the tenth time that day (and the morning had barely even started according to her standards). The document had last been altered and saved at 4:45 a.m. that morning.

With a sigh, she decided to analyze the facts with less drama. She'd write down the three lines that intended to close out Beta's sexual chapter and would sleep for a few more hours. It was all she needed. But she couldn't find chapter 13 in the document. "Beta's version" was written in its place.

She read all 904 words at lightning speed and took pride in the fact that her drunkenness had inspired her. The character was rebelling against the author's dominance and rewrote the chapter. She began to think that sleep-writing was the best. Or her subconscious, alter ego, other personality, whoever or whatever induced her to write those lines.

While rereading everything calmly, she noticed some Spanish words that were not in her vocabulary. Words that were a bit too…sexual for someone who barely had sex with a Spanish man in real life. Had she been watching too many erotic films? She wouldn't confess that so willingly.

Her phone vibrated. There were new notifications on Facebook. This time, there were comments on her new picture. "Picture?" Her forehead scrunched as she logged on.

"Oh fuuuuuuuuuuuuck!" she said out loud.

That picture had to have been photoshopped or faked, even. She thought about calling the police and deleting her account. She was fuming, but didn't know at whom.

She looked again. It wasn't her in the picture. Or was it? Hugging a guy from behind to cause intrigue. With that came millions of curious comments. The image should be deleted or not? "Maybe my laptop has been hacked and a person has gained remote access" was Alberta's only explanation that made sense. She took the opportunity to save her new book to a flash drive just in case. Something still bothered her, and she just found out why.

"What the hell is going on!? Why is my book switched to third person, narrating my reactions, and referring to me as Alberta? Where did this fucking narrator come from???" She lost control, using language that was more explicit than usual.

She couldn't believe that a fantasy author had taken over her book. It was too bizarre. Her title switched from Deceit to *Beta Version.*

"What do you mean?" the ex-author begged. "Ex? There's no way…"

Alberta almost fell back when she saw *her* following post, this time through a photo app on her phone. The image had been posted for over 10,000 followers on Instagram and another 15,000 on Twitter.

The caption said: "Miguel Angelo, my new Spanish fling."

Rapidly searching the minibar for more sparkling water, only to find she had already drunk them all. Deciding to go with a beer, she chugged it all at once to try and swallow the most recent information. Her logical thinking had halted. It took a while for things to sink in, and her brain slowly started working again in small bursts, somewhat like this:

"It wasn't my picture. Whoever she is, Beta was hugging my Miguelangelo, I'm almost sure. The Spanish guy that I met in Bahia two years ago. But maybe the written way of his name is separated: Miguel Angelo. Yeah, it seems to be the same guy from our past, but with a beard. Yes, and I guess that now he is a married family man. Oh, that bitch broke my golden rule! And everyone thinks I am her and she is me. So they think I'm going out with a married man. Am I? No!!! I haven't fucked anyone in over two months!" she frantically remembered.

Either the world had gone crazy, or she was already drunk again. Or both. Or worse, because mixing alcohol and cold medicine was never a good idea. She considered taking the whole box of pills, but remembered she was hidden and no one could rescue her in time.

On second glance, Alberta noticed the picture had a localization pin at the *Plaza de la Cibeles*. She decided to call *Praktik Metropol*, the hotel she had reserved in Madrid, pretending to be someone else and asking about herself, Alberta, or Beta.

As suspected, the concierge confirmed that she *was* staying there but was out at the moment and that her account already had two charges. Whoever was messing with her was actually in Madrid.

Alberta decided it was time to go there.

She tried to delete the pictures from her social media, but *someone* had already changed her password. It wouldn't take long for Miguel's wife to discover the affair. Al would keep the guilt and shame without having enjoyed any of the good sex, beyond the verbal, of course.

"Good one, Beta! This is how you repay me?" she thought, full of hate.

Al found herself at the LATAM boarding gate in Guarulhos again. She spent the equivalent of all of the Christmas gifts she had planned on buying on the trip on a last-minute red-eye flight from São Paulo to Madrid.

She looked wild. Smudged makeup in the corner of her eyes, gnawed nails, and the sloppiness of someone who believed they would be hidden for ten days. Not a single lipstick in her purse. She had checked her toiletry bag into her small suitcase alongside all her shoes, books, and a backup flash drive with her new story saved. She always backed things up twice just in case.

Narrowly avoiding being accused of fraud, she spent more than half an hour explaining that she hadn't boarded the first flight, even wishing she had a fake passport, the kind that's always readily available in fiction.

She tried to picture herself in different circumstances. Still, now that she actually needed it, she could only visualize herself in an asylum, stuck in a straitjacket, smiling because of the effect of the potent sedatives.

She hated traveling in economy. Four days ago, she had put Beta in her first-class seat, and now all that was left was a seat in the middle row of the plane. The crying kids did not help either. Peeing in a bathroom for a hundred people—don't even mention it. She wished she had been born with a bigger bladder.

Maybe the exhaustion she felt contradicted the rule. She took a deep breath, turned up the volume of her headphones, and decided to surrender as she listened to The Killers loudly playing to drown out her predicament. The circumstances always improved when she pretended to be ignorant, or it was best to think that was indeed the case.

Her phone remained unanswered. She texted her mom and daughter to let them know she would be unreachable for 24 hours. Deep down, she wanted to disappear for days, but figured hours would be more reasonable.

She dreamt of infinite Russian dolls; once she opened one, more Betas were inside. The game was dizzying, and Al started to doubt her own existence.

Once she landed, she patiently waited for her second suitcase, the one with the books and the shoes, and the conveyor belt stopped spinning. Of course, her luggage was lost.

Day Five

Alberta arrived in Madrid exhausted, realizing she probably hadn't carried enough coats.

She took subway lines 8, 4, and 1 to get to the *Gran Via.* On the last leg, she chose precisely the cart where highly animated accordion players filled the otherwise silent air. It felt like the slowest subway ride of her life. All she needed was a flamenco dancer to round out the day, and she was sure she would run into one eventually.

Sitting in front of her on the subway was a Spanish woman of the same age, but beautiful, retouching her makeup. "As if she needed it", she thought ironically. Al searched for her reflection on the glass door, but what she saw was a pale person with bright fluorescent red hair, clean, yet a little untidy. She kept comparing her chances of enchanting someone in this state. It's a good thing she wasn't good with numbers.

There wasn't a single book to distract herself with, but she remembered a tale by Cortázar that took place on the Paris subway based on a game he had made up. It was about waiting for the subway car's window to give him an answer. The happiness that comes from an encounter at the intersection of gazes.

"Finally, Madrid", she thought. She arrived five days after what was initially planned, with no shoes, interesting books, toiletries, and…

"My God! My book!" She said out loud, attracting the attention of the passengers. Her backup flash drive had also been lost. At least the situation couldn't get any worse. Or could it?

There she went, disconnected, alienated, out of shape, looking for someone she's not sure even exists. She'd grown unaccustomed to searching for things lately. Everything arrived for her before she could even want it. People always told her where they were, sent invites, scheduled meetings, and responded promptly. Everything was always dissected for her; she just had to decide if she wanted it or not. But now, all she had was this story with its cold and weird city.

Dragging her carry-on bag through the subway station, she made her way up to the little hotel. In the elevator, she stood still as she tried to figure out where she should go. There were three hotels in the same building, and it took some time to locate the correct reception desk.

"*Buenos días*!" she said to the concierge.

"*Hola señora*, I thought you had switched hotels?"

Alberta didn't know what to say, but reminded herself to act naturally, no matter how hard it was. "Don't drop the ball now", she thought.

"Did I? No, no. So… I'd like to reopen my bill."

"Unfortunately, we don't have any more rooms available. We have a literary event in the city tomorrow, and all the hotels in the building are fully booked."

"Huh…Okay, *gracias*." She said, unsure if she had already canceled her panel at the event. She was unsure of herself and of where to go. Beta ran away before she could arrive, and Al thought it was best to look for a hotel closest to the *Plaza de las Cibeles*.

That was when the concierge remembered something and called her back.

Beta laughed while trying to imagine Alberta arriving in Madrid, completely bewildered. She knew she would come since she couldn't handle losing control of her book or of her reputation. It was a ridiculous notion that could only be explained by the fact that Al had isolated herself too much from the world to notice it.

How is it possible that she could have assimilated so much into virtual life? She no longer turned the TV on for information or pleasure, not even to watch her favorite pastime of soccer. She rarely left the house. She read a book per week, often forgot to eat, and abandoned all the sports she had previously practiced. She aged more and more each day and became uninteresting.

It was hard on Julia, who ended up siding with her dad. He took advantage of the situation by being excessively affectionate with the girl as a way to punish Alberta or make her jealous of the bond he had with their daughter.

"Alberta needed an eye-opener like this. Perhaps an even bigger one?" Beta grinned, brimming with ideas. After all, accessing experiences instead of references was much richer for a writer. "Who knows? A handsome Spanish man would help alleviate parts of the problem. Maybe she wouldn't have so many golden rules, critiques, and wounds that seemed never to heal."

Before leaving the hotel room to meet Miguel in Atocha, Beta spread out some messages that Al would eventually find at the right time. If Al didn't know how to live, Beta knew it fully for both of them.

"I always do what I want", Beta repeated the affirmation to herself as a mantra.

"It's impossible for my plans to go wrong", she thought. At this point, Alberta had already received the notes she left at the hotel.

Al was jet-lag personified. As Alice in Wonderland, she looked at the crazy watch on her wrist and didn't know if it was four hours ahead or behind. The biting wind invaded the tiny holes in her coat. All she wanted was to wrap herself under a blanket immediately, but she couldn't.

Her "new pseudo author" left a note at the hotel's reception desk saying, EAT ME. She thought this had to have been some sort of insane joke. Beta went as far as scheduling a lunch with Lucia at *Cerveceria 100 Montalditos*. Al looked at the note and sighed out of exasperation.

It was so close that when she asked, the concierge took her to the reception window and pointed at a charming spot on the other side of the street full of people sitting on the sidewalk. Even on a day when the thermometers marked 51°F, the restaurant was lively with the crowd. She crossed the street with her suitcase in hand (she wouldn't let it out of her sight for any reason, as if holding on to her own life). Still disoriented by that new world, she found herself playing a character of herself with no free will. She lacked the energy or desire to react to any of it.

Upon arrival, she found a worried Lucia. "Was I late? Very much so", she found out. She explained it was because of the lost suitcase without getting into too much detail.

Al was starving. She couldn't remember her last meal, as she had refused to eat during the flight. The smell of Spanish olive oil excited her senses with its nutty smell that followed its clean distinct warmth of spicy tones, perfect somehow in sparking a warmth in this weather. Without noticing, she smiled immediately after biting into her first tapa and found the Spanish *jamón* divine, as if she was again reconnecting with the real life's simple pleasures. She ate about five large tapas and drank three glasses of wine. Her friend warned her that the wine wasn't the best. Al said the worst Spanish wine still seemed pleasing to her Brazilian palate.

Lucia was a psychologist with no kids and three Spanish ex-husbands. Alberta took the opportunity to ask her about schizophrenia. Her friend questioned her about her new story, and soon the conversation drifted away from the topic. Multiple personalities? Amnesia? Hallucinogenic drugs that she'd sometimes unintentionally digest in a club in *Baixo Augusta*?

Maybe Lucia didn't believe all the madness. Alberta, being exaggerating, was used to using her friends and acquaintances as laboratories for her articles, tales, and stories, feeding her knowledge for her own books and stories. The idea that someone had hacked her social media accounts was more credible, even though the story she told on impulse, with a mouthful of food and slightly intoxicated, was quite incredible. Or unbelievable. Maybe even a bit of both.

Lucia laughed while checking her phone, and Alberta wanted to know what was so funny.

"Fake you just posted a picture of the view from your new hotel in Madrid."

Beta had posted a picture on Twitter of the *Plaza de las Cibeles* view through the window of a beautiful apartment that Alberta imagined was Miguel's. With the bill arrived a key with an address printed on a metal key chain. Now, Al had a place to stay.

Beta realized the sun had come out from the rays that entered the cracks of the Atocha. It was a winter sun that did little to warm things up, but it brightened up the space.

The city was getting into the end-of-the-year rhythm she noticed when she smoked outside. Hastened pedestrians with gift bags and buses with messages of *año nuevo*. She went back to the station to wait for her train. Which one would it be?

Her neck was hurting from looking up at the iron and glass structure of the atrium that protected the tropical greenhouse in the middle of the city. The project that had the help of Gustave Eiffel and his team, a fact she later learned from Miguel.

"What a beautiful day it is, right, Al? This proves that Madrid wants you here. Take care of everything, dear," She smiled while waiting for her tea to cool down, seated at a small kiosk that served the executives who passed by every day. It was ideal for resting by a comforting heater, people watching, and listening in on conversations.

Alone, and realizing that she wasn't a content person, she searched for conversation, smiled at everyone, wanting to connect with the world, searching for a simple *hola*, an indication, or a comment. Small things with all types of people to feel a little bit of humanity.

Beta ordered a brownie. Learned to walk slower, and to eat *muy* slowly, because with the cold, the ice cream that came with the brownie took a while to melt. And that was a good thing. She didn't need to kill time with bullets. She would make it die smiling, thinking everything was worth it, what some might call *la dolce vita.*

This magical moment was interrupted by her observation that 60% of the Spanish used Neymar's haircut. Alberta had noticed that as well. She was a soccer fanatic but stopped writing about it a long time ago and no longer attends the games.

Beta didn't understand the rapidly spoken Spanish, but imagined that at the neighboring table, the deal of the century was being closed. Two older gentlemen on one side, listening to two on the other (so cute that she would readily accept their resumes). The younger and *guapo* ones tried to convince the others to accept a proposal, using drawings made on napkins. The older ones responded with questioning faces and pauses for strategic analysis. She rooted for the younger ones to win the dispute and to celebrate on top of her.

Now they wrote numbers on paper with many zeros. It was best to stop speculating, as they already were eyeing her. The waiter also walked around with an expression that said, "I can't believe she's been eating this brownie for 40 minutes." In the lobby, she saw a million people hugging each other, goodbyes, reunions, flower bouquets, and a heater that was capable of melting hearts.

"Last call for Toledo," she heard in a heavy Spanish accent coming from the speakers. On the board, there were trains to Alicante in five minutes and to Barcelona. Huge advertising incentivized the Spanish people to go visit Mexico, "*Aún Hoy*".

She took advantage of being early and walked around the station, uncertain if they would go to Toledo or Escorial. Miguel spoke a lot about both cities and wanted to take her to the *Charoles* restaurant in the latter, where he'd had the best *cocido* in the world. When Beta heard that he decided to go to Toledo, she sighed in relief. The pictures she had seen of those *cocidos* in Escorial online didn't seem that appetizing.

On the phone, Miguel asked her to leave the station. They would be driving there instead, and he was already waiting at the entrance. Beta was upset she didn't get to ride a Spanish train, but the trip would be more intimate this way.

He was probably up to something, but it was of her nature to trust without hesitation.

Al was a tiny red-headed ant with a red suitcase sitting next to the fountain at the *Plaza de las Cibeles*. She felt minuscule, as if being watched from Miguel's apartment window, exactly as she had described in her character's sexual chapter. "So that apartment really existed?" She was curious to know what she had gotten right when she wrote about him, and at the same time, her legs refused to pursue it.

Would she find Beta up there? If she didn't see her, was it really all just a trick? She thought being a character was less complicated. Maybe Al wasn't good at this, since she overanalyzed the facts and got stuck on the "decline the call" part. Resigned, she sighed and dragged her suitcase to the building.

It was impossible not to think about sex as she entered the elevator. Had they filmed it? Did the doorman smile maliciously, thinking that Al and Beta were the same person? She blushed thinking about it. It's best not to blame herself for what others have done.

It was a small but impressive penthouse. Very organized and masculine based on the tone of brown chosen for the walls, which contrasted with red and black objects. Everything was so Spanish, but at the same time, nothing as heavy as it could've been with the color choices.

Standing at the entrance, deciding what to do, she was, in fact, alone, which became clear when ringing the doorbell three times with no response. A low meow flooded the air, and she instantly noticed a fat yellow cat as it weaved between her legs. This time she wasn't frightened, but happy with the company, which was more appealing than the company of many people. She smiled, bending down and noticing a name printed on its collar: CHESIRE.

“Oh, so you're the one giving my Alice all these crazy ideas?” she asked, picking him up. He smiled, as if confirming the joke, and jumped to introduce her to the apartment. She felt as if she had definitely lost her mind once and for all.

From the living room, Al followed him through the tiny kitchen, which probably had never been used, through the office covered in papers, until they arrived at the central room of the house—a fantastic suite. Alberta stopped at the door, and the cat meowed from inside, inviting her to enter.

She didn't find a guest room or a pullout sofa for guests, and decided to go back to the living room, in search of some sort of message or clue about her next step. "Was Beta suggesting that I sleep on Miguel's bed? I hate staying in other people's houses, let alone their bed."

Moving about, the enchantment of Miguel's books made her completely forget what she was looking for. Books of different genres, contemporary Spanish authors she's always wanted to read, classics, and many Brazilian authors adorned the shelves. Opening some of the works, she noticed many thoughtful dedications to "the famous publisher." She hoped she would be able to read some of those books during her stay.

Feeling smaller, watched by the cat from the top of the bookshelf, she wondered when she would be of her normal size again.

Through the window, she saw small couples embracing tightly in the square. They took thousands of pictures of the fountain, the monument, and the night. She needed to spend money. Retail therapy always seemed to alleviate her loneliness. She would buy an entirely new toiletry bag with so much makeup that she would never use. It was a form of collecting. She imagined parties and circumstances, cutting out references from fashion magazines, but preferred to incorporate all of that into her characters. Real life didn't reach her imagination. Like a book that gets adapted into a film. It often loses its joy and impact.

Whenever she was forced to live in the real world, she tried to distort it, so it seemed friendlier or less dangerous. One day, Julia forced her to swim with dolphins at a waterpark. She only relaxed when she convinced herself the animal was just a robot programmed to trick tourists.

She went back to looking at the living room and found an open laptop with the beginning of a chapter detailing Beta's plans. She would meet up with Miguel for a quick train ride to a nearby city. Even if Alberta wanted to, she wouldn't have enough time to stop it. Their meeting would have to take place another day.

Al really missed writing. Some urgent ideas continued to be added to a parallel document to be used in the next chapters, and her competitive side began to show signs of life. She needed to get back at Beta.

After getting some water in the kitchen, she came back and found another card she hadn't noticed before. In it, there was the name of a bar and a time written down, suggesting Al's next step.

"*DRINK ME*. Have fun and take care of yourself." She realized the note was actually saying, "Figure it out yourself." "A little bit of autonomy, Beta? *Gracias*, dear. You don't lose by waiting," she laughed with Cheshire. She was starting to like this little double game.

"How wonderful it is being a character," Beta thought as her long blond hair danced in the wind that invaded the car. She wasn't cold, she didn't have to use a condom, she could drink and drive, and she could surpass the speed limit without getting any tickets. Fiction's backbone was quite soft.

They became fond of the car in front that opened up a path for them, and joked that they would follow it onto the highway. The sunny day made all the pictures look beautiful. They devised word games that distorted their meaning, while Miguel taught Beta every type of curse word in Spanish.

In Spain, if she were to say she wanted *pinga*, a Brazilian alcohol, she would get a penis instead, a funny miscommunication. The similarities in the words *cuello* (neck) and *culo* (ass) would also generate a lot of confusion, especially when in bed.

Miguel was a fantastic guy, and Beta knew he would get his own chapter if Al met him. He shared his insane intellectual baggage inherited from a fervent generation of readers. While listening to him on the phone with his friends, she turned into a child who listened to adults speaking in a language she didn't understand. He knew so much about so many things, always had a good story to tell, and collected important contacts that held him in high esteem. He was truly a person to fall in love with, if only Beta were someone who fell in love easily. But she couldn't run that risk.

She felt as if she saw herself on the other side of the highway, passing by on the way back to Madrid in an identical car to the one they were in. She was born with that dejà vu, as if she always crossed paths with other versions of herself that had made different choices.

Maybe it was the impatient Beta who took the train in Atocha because she couldn't wait for Miguel. Or another version of her and another Miguel who went to Escorial to eat the best *cocido* in the world. Maybe it was the Beta that ran away with the Miguelangelo she met in *Morro de São Paulo* two years ago. "Do these other versions of us live out adventures in parallel worlds?" She was dying to know.

Sex bomb by Tom Jones was playing on the radio, and she started to tease Miguel, who drove faster and faster to get there sooner. They quickly arrived to finish what they had slowly begun doing in the car.

The Hotel *El Cigarral de las Mercedes* was situated on the outskirts of the city, located within a historic villa at the top of a hill. It was inevitable to think of the most recent *Almodóvar* movie that had taken place there, with Antonio Banderas playing a sadistic doctor who toys with the identity of his patient.

Beta smoked her cigarette after a quickie, with plumes of smoke sparking a wish that Al could also have fun on her first night in Madrid. She eventually looked over at Miguel, curious to see if this man whose chest moved up and down with each breath actually existed or if he was also a fictional character.

Alberta finished another chapter. She didn't write it on the apartment's laptop, so there would be no risk to her story. She had already lost the first-person narrative and a flash drive inside a suitcase. She wasn't going to spread her story anymore through those random machines.

It was time to clear her head and do some shopping at the *Plaza Puerta del Sol.* A good shower was much needed, and in Miguel's bathroom, she wasn't going to find anything to get ready for the night. After everything that had happened, Alberta deserved some fun without having to lie or hide. Or maybe she'd be able to lie even more.

The beautiful day invited everyone out into the streets. She decided to walk up to the *Gran Via* and then down to *Puerta del Sol,* following the same path as before, passing by her hotel again. She had the habit of liking what was known. If allowed, she'd most likely walk through those same streets for the rest of her trip, would eat the same tapas, and drink the same wine from lunch. Alberta felt disappointed because she had yet to see any of the prostitutes described in her book. They probably started working later, she thought.

She answered Carlos on her phone, who wanted to know about her panel. "Oh, right. The panel." She had forgotten to prepare anything about what to say tomorrow, but there was also not much to prepare. She considered sharing the story of an author who lost her book to her character, but figured that wouldn't be very credible despite her current reality.

Carlos laughed at her new story, "So those beautiful pictures on Facebook were just pretend? You have a big imagination, Al." Carlos said condescendingly. She changed the subject. Her Brazilian editor was one of those old bachelors we'd never know if they were gay or too friendly and respectful.

Her friends would always say that he flirted with Alberta, but it was all so discreet that she always thought it was moral support rather than anything else.

In the store's fitting room, she noticed how much weight she had lost in the last couple of days. Everything she picked up in her usual size was now too loose. "Too much sex," she laughed ironically, choosing a dress with a much lower neckline than her usual standards. No one there knew her anyway. As she filled up a giant bag with beauty products, it was already getting dark.

Miguel's bathtub was no less than that of a five-star hotel. Oh, how she wanted to lie there eternally, drinking a glass of kava that she found with her name written on it in the fridge. "If all of this is just a prank, please don't let it stop now", she implored in thought. Cheshire smiled slyly. He rested on the face towel on the sink. It was ironic how he was always above her head. Was it easier to read her thoughts that way?

The night was way too cold for the dress she purchased, even wearing a topcoat. She searched for a club whose name she couldn't remember, and decided to ask the prostitutes who, at that time, had flooded the street of her ex-hotel.

First, they stared at her suspiciously. But it only took one second for them to realize Al wasn't much of a threat. They lit their cigarettes and discussed the crisis Spain was facing, due to the devaluation of its currency, which had increased the frequency of free blow jobs. Those women deserved government recognition for the consolation they provided to the poor workers and the unemployed Spanish population.

Following the suggestion of her new friends, she ended up in a spot called *Boite*. "*Hay un concerto hoy?*" The hostess quickly informed her. "Who's playing?" but the doorman shrugged. Al decided to pay the eight euros to go in. She received a stamp on her hand and entered a hot, dark space filled with people. She didn't regret it in the slightest.

It seemed like one of those perfect nights to drink as much as possible and be carried out by her friends. Was she becoming addicted to alcohol? Also, she was aware that she was alone and should at least make two new friends before she blacked out. Hopefully, she chose the strongest and friendliest ones.

Soul music of the highest quality was playing. She drank vodka and Sprite, danced without stopping, used the men's bathroom (there wasn't a sign!), and found a new friend open to escort her in case she drank too much. And even if she didn't drink at all. "Was this one of Beta's friends?"

Alberta took a long time to realize that she was being flirted with by her new and pretty friend, Helena. It only clicked when Helena was already whispering suggestively in her ear, with her hand deep in the root of her hair. Was the dress to blame? As she decided whether she wanted to let the situation evolve, Al received some neck kisses and felt as if she could approach it using her old dolphin tactic. Was her imagination powerful? All she had to do was think about a hot guy, ignore the voice, and relax. But when the kissing scene arrived, she saw that reality was not more powerful than fiction. There was a beard missing, and hormones were missing. She needed the Y chromosome. She kindly said goodbye, recomposed herself, and left.

Many of her friends had spoken highly of the experience. Maybe she hadn't had enough to drink, but if all meaning were hidden in lesbian sex, she would be missing out, she decided.

Day Six

The sun was rising, and Miguel took advantage of the trip to schedule a meeting at the University of Toledo. Something about a competition for young writers, if Beta had understood it correctly. Does he still intend to return to Madrid for Alberta's lecture today? Beta hoped not. She wanted to stay one more night in that incredible place. And based on how things were going, it didn't seem that hard to convince him.

She wandered the cold streets of Toledo. The sun seemed weaker, and the shadows on the tiny streets colder. She listened to the *Bruna Caram* singer play loudly through her headphones as she wandered around the old houses, observing their iron balconies with perfectly hydraulic tiles when viewed from below. In all the windows, there were medieval armories and small statues of *Don Quixote*.

With Cervantes in mind, Beta decided she needed some "salt in the head" and waited for Miguel in the garden of a small pub on the street of the university, right in front of St. Thomas' church. She wasn't very knowledgeable about sacred art and had little interest in the *El Greco* piece, which had been in the church since its construction. She'd eat some tapas in the meantime and would later go up the tower with Miguel, only for the impressive view that they offered of the hills.

The sun was colder than her white wine, and many small birds were surrounding her. That sun, that music, that wine. Sleepiness, a good hangover, and numb thoughts. She liked life like this. Light was a word full of meaning.

It didn't take long for Miguel to appear, energized from his time with the young adults who shared his love for literature. He confessed he was too lazy to return to Madrid just for the panel today. He mentioned Alberta, a talented Brazilian writer, who was known as a grumpy old woman. Beta laughed and asked if he had ever seen her. Not that he knew or remembered, he guessed he only knew her book, which he wanted to represent in Madrid.

Beta already knew that, among all the Miguels in the city, the Angelo who was trying to contact to publish Alberta's book was the same Miguelangelo they had met 2 years ago. Beta decided to tell him about Al, after all, she was in his home. However, she only shared the bare minimum, like a "what if" reality of the facts. Miguel was serious as he listened to Beta's story. He lit a cigarette and smoked slowly before sharing his thoughts on everything he had just heard. After a while, he smiled and decided to "remain" in that crazy story, as weird as it seemed. "What a chance to be author and character of their stories at the same time," he thought.

What Miguel didn't know was that he would be helping Beta with a weird plan to make Al's panel a little more fun. After all, it was time to inspire her author. Beta predicted that Miguel would like what was going to happen later.

In Madrid, nightmares shook Alberta out of bed way too early.

The ancient and remote past still breathed down her neck with the breath of a jaguar. It was Christmas shopping day for the family. She needed to handle the packages soon to get rid of that responsibility. *El Corte Inglés* seemed like the perfect option.

Strangely, the chocolate croissant didn't sit well in her stomach, and she had to enter the fitting room of the first store she saw to remove some layers as she was burning up, even though it was 50°F.

There were more beggars on her path than usual, which stirred up a familiar agony. Department stores with Christmas music made the terrible experience even worse. To top it all off, the Christmas music was religious in nature.

It all started with a strange stiff neck. Many helpful sellers were offering her coupons. Her mixture of Spanish, Portuguese, and English only worsened throughout the day, and her mouth went slack. Was her blood pressure low? She still needed to get a couple of presents on two different floors. She started to walk faster, feeling the bags getting way too heavy.

"Listo! Por favor, dónde es la salida del inferno?"

"Cómo?"

"La salida!"

The cold air aided in her panic as drops of sweat trickled down her forehead. The world was way too bright. Counting three blocks to the apartment, all she wanted to do was kneel on the sidewalk and put her forehead on the ground. But someone was already doing exactly that, holding a piece of cardboard saying they had four children and no money. She carried three giant bags and was out of breath. Guilty of her white people's problems.

She followed an extensive line that spanned two blocks and went into a lottery store. "Santa Claus can't handle all that hope", she lamented. She arrived in the room dizzy. She threw the bags on the floor and her body on the bed. Vertigo, or is she living inside a dream?

"What did I come here for again? I found out that traveling solo isn't that fun. Beautiful couples laugh loudly, very close to my ears. And the worst part is that Madrid is romantic. All I want to do is call the event organizers, claiming to have some sort of infectious disease."

She would try her best not to take that story an inch further. Stretched out on the couch of that incredible apartment with a yellow cat on her lap, she just wanted to see if the narrative was capable of reaching her.

Alberta had been siestaing for half an hour when Miguel's abandoned laptop made a sound. Cheshire was the first to get up. Al waited for the noise to persist, predicting this was another of Beta's tricks. Bingo! Finally, she was online. It was disappointing that there wasn't an image available, as she was crazy to see the character she desperately wanted to murder.

"Oh, there you are, Al!"

"Yes, so game over."

"The real question is, what will you do now with your favorite character? Hahaha."

"Identity theft charges? I don't think that's enough."

"Hahaha. You're fun, Alberta."

"Ok. Now I want to know who you are."

"I'm the person you want to be. The one who's not afraid of living."

"Alright, that's enough, you shitty hacker!"

"What's the problem, Al? Just because you're bad with technology doesn't mean you're being monitored. You could even call me a heteronym, right? Either way, I'm you. Or should I say, I'm us? Hahaha."

"I want to see you laughing in jail."

"Sure. I want to see you report us to the police and admit that your trip was all a lie and that you used the publisher's money on top of that."

"I'm here now, aren't I?"

"Thanks to me, you mean?"

"I thought I at least had free will."

"It was clever of you to convince the world that you were here. Maybe you wouldn't have even come."

"And you did your dirty work while I wasn't here, didn't you? You shitty little romantic. Did you need to hook up with a married guy?"

"Failed marriages don't count… It was a good trick, wasn't it?"

"It better have been!"

"Don't worry. Nothing much happened." Beta lied. "I had to get you to come, and it worked!"

"Low blow. I hope there's still time to fix everything. Speaking of which, where are you? I want my life back!"

"It's about time you got out of your coma. A little bit of cold air on your face. I also got some good deals for us, a more advantageous translation and distribution contract, as well as confirmation of tonight's panel, which you had previously tried to get out of."

"Nice. I hope you planned out the talk too."

"Actually, I was thinking about talking about this real vs. virtual game we've been playing. There's been so much confusion over this. The truth is, you're just a cowardly writer, hahahaha."

"Cowardly or tired, you don't understand anything."

"You have a career. A career you pursued and chose over your marriage, and now you just want to neglect it."

"Who are you to lecture me? An imposter, a reader, someone who's jealous? Do you really think I'm going to fall for this? What are you even getting out of this?"

"I'm you, sweetheart. And we both know that. I'm just a bit smarter, hahahahahaha."

"Those posts on my Facebook page were ridiculous."

"Sorry, I was drunk and quite excited…"

"I have a daughter who sees everything on there, damn it!"

"Ok. Your Facebook has been cleared, and I promise to control myself from now on."

"I bet the lesbian friend was your idea, too."

"Hahahahahaha. And I bet you ran away!"

"You really have a death wish, huh?"

"Listen. To redeem myself, I've planned an inspiring discussion for today's panel. I know you can't stand talking about literature anymore, but I swear I will help today. From a distance and virtually. Wanna bet?"

"No, I don't want to."

"Come on, think about it. Everything is already done, and we'll be watching the event here from Toledo."

"I thought you were in Escorial."

"That doesn't matter. I promise it will be the most incredible experience you've had in a while. All you have to do is follow my advice and say the word 'fake' into the microphone."

"And what if I don't want to?"

"You'll miss out on an amazing adventure. If you want to end the experience, say 'real,' and everything will return to normal, okay?"

"I don't understand what your game is."

"There is no game. I just think it'd be a great idea to talk about me and your new book tonight. People will go crazy! And as a reward, you'll also freak out a bit with what I told you to do. 'Fake' and 'real' are your magic words. Say them as many times as you'd like. Don't forget it!"

"Duh… Do you think I'm stupid?"

"Just a little, haha. I have to go. *Hasta la vista*!"

"Hey, wait."

The connection has ended.

According to Beta, Miguel would not be at the lecture. There was so much chaos here, and Al imagined it was the same in Toledo.

The auditorium was packed, and Al remembered that she hadn't brought her single book, the object that had made her famous and earned her an invitation to speak on that stage before 300 people. But what were 300 people to someone who had 15,000 followers? "They're real. They're from another country, and they hadn't even read her book in their language! Get ready to kill time, Alberta", she said to herself, already predicting trouble.

The opening panel consisted of herself, a well-known moderator to the audience, and a contemporary Spanish author whom she had never heard of. Which was better, so she wouldn't fan girl on stage. His name was Pablo something, and he spoke about the literary social media *platform megustaescribir.com,* where he had just debuted as an author.

They started with some basic questions about the writing process, the discipline needed, and so on. They asked Al what her experience was writing her debut novel. The same question was directed to the young writer next to her, and Al could barely understand his slang-filled modern Spanish. Her mind was miles away from there, imagining Beta and Miguel somewhere in a hotel room watching her speak. Were they actually watching? She felt an itch and decided to bring the conversation to her next project and say the words that "Beta the Mage" had given her.

To her luck, the next question was about writer's block and how the success of a first book can weigh on a writer to the point where they take a while to release their next one. Al took the microphone and said that she hadn't experienced any problems and had already started writing a new novel ordered by her publisher.

"… A book that challenges the limits of what is fake and–"

Al started losing her voice. Suddenly, where the audience was, it seemed to be a giant holographic screen with a couple having sex as in *Chatroulette*, and Beta stared at Al out of the corner of her eye. "There's no way Miguel had agreed to that!" The astonishment lasted for a second or two before Al regained her words, "...which is real". Distressingly, she looked for a cup of water at the end of her sentence, not being able to hide her shock.

"How was a connection like that possible? Did the development team from Apple choose me as a guinea pig? Or was this one of those biotechnology experiments that I always see on TEDx? Maybe an optical illusion from Aleph, a Tesseract, magic, something supernatural? How is it possible that no one else saw that scene?!"

The conversation continued, and Pablo asked Alberta a question, which she asked to be repeated. She should have been paying attention to respond, but her brain could only think about adding the magic words into her answer. Al cursed herself for not having practiced at home, since she knew of this game before it even started.

She felt like Beta, and the world that watched online must have been laughing at her. Or not? Al was skilled in the art of disguising her feelings. Pablo waited for her answer, and she began sharing how she had conceived the idea for her new book and how much technology can track what people do nowadays if they're naive enough to overexpose themselves. It could also be a tool of manipulation, allowing one person to influence others into believing exactly what they wanted.

"You mix the universes of what is fake and real," she finished saying.

There was another flash. What an insane experience. It almost seemed sensorial. She needed a bigger interval between both words, she thought, anxious for the next question. The moderator said that they would be taking questions from anyone who wanted to submit them through Twitter. "She wouldn't be capable of interrupting what was happening for this. Or would she?"

She heard the moderator say that writer Rodrigo Fresán published in a Spanish newspaper, that every writer has four lives: the public, the private, the books they write, and those they read. He asked her if she used that theory in her book. Time to answer, Alberta.

"I think it's more complex than that. It's as if I wanted to bring the worlds together through comparison and questioning of what we consider fake today," she paused and could see, feel, and hear the music that screamed alongside Beta.

It felt strange being an observer of that scene, but she was also curious. She hoped no one knew what she was watching, which added an extra layer of enjoyment because it felt secretive. She then remembered technology was almost at the point of guessing our thoughts and posting on social media everything we read or click. A sense of dread ran through her body, and she quickly regained her composure, interrupting Pablo, who had already started to speak, apologizing after and chugging all of her water in one swift gulp.

Despite the confusion, the audience was captivated by the story Al told, which was both dramatic and confusing. The moderator then opened the floor for questions from the public, and a somewhat hipster, skinny teenager wanted to know where her character was.

"She's kind of a nymphomaniac, so I wouldn't doubt it if she were having a lot more fun than I am right now."

The statement took the audience aback, as gasps and exclamations filled the air.

The moderator interrupted the manifestation to ask if there was any chance her character was called Beta. Al confirmed, and the moderator explained that Beta had just sent a note to the author, requesting the production team to project it on the wall.

@beta Al, dear, you almost ruined the mood, but we had already climaxed. At the same time. ;P

The audience applauded what they considered to be a perfectly synchronized marketing tactic, while the moderator claimed that the entirety of Spain would be anxiously awaiting her new novel.

An incredible idea on how to attract Beta dawned on Al. In her closing statement, she announced that her character would attend the autograph session at the book fair the following day. The TV network requested an interview, but Al said they would have to wait till the following afternoon, as Beta would be a much more interesting character.

Now the story was public. Beta had the opportunity to tarnish her reputation further. Or not. Al figured she should trust her more. After all, her character was having a lot more fun than she imagined.

In Toledo, Miguel, who knew that the ladies' lives did not intersect, felt strange. He always dreamed of having sex with two women, but never imagined he would feel so watched. What happened to the good old classic *menage à trois*?

It was late into the night, and Al didn't even think about going to bed. She needed to recap every event and try to bring some order to the chaos that was happening in her head. She couldn't find a rational explanation for it all. But she also didn't want to believe that Beta was just her character that had come to life, even if it was only Al who had seen the scene.

"Yes, she does, in fact, exist. And she's kind of similar to me, except for getting caught in such an intimate moment. Yes, she was crazy for exposing herself in that way". She opened the laptop and went to Google to try to find any new technology that could explain the parallel world she accessed. Nothing. Could it be in a testing phase?

Her phone started to vibrate with messages from Carlos, and that's when she noticed she had 14 missed calls from him. On WhatsApp, he commented on the panel's exceptional impact, which people hadn't cared about in the first place, and that two more publishers in Spain were fighting with Angelo over the rights to her second book, good one.

Carlos couldn't type anymore because he was getting on a plane, but would arrive in time for dinner tomorrow with Al and Angelo, who will come from Toledo just for this event.

The inner thoughts of Alberta seemed to scream: "Wait, wait, wait, so Miguel Angelo, the Beta's lover and owner of this apartment, is the same Miguelangelo from Bahia? Oh my God, I had a fling with Angelo, this important publisher, two years ago and didn't even know it? All this time, with all the Spanish men named Miguel, the Spanish Publisher who is trying to contact me (and using his second name Angelo) is the very same man who helped me to get over my divorce? What are the odds?

Did he agree to mess with my life through Beta? Or worse: I'm not the only one playing the game author x character, and he created Beta based on the synopsis of my next book that I had sent for him months ago? Or Miguel would send over Angelo, his author?"

Cheshire laughed at her confusion. She needed to digest all of that. Through the large windows, she watched a deserted Madrid.

Day Seven

Beta awoke alone. Miguel's note indicated that he thought he could be part of their crazy story, but the last chapter left him feeling very uncomfortable. She could tell he felt used, but Beta knew he would have never agreed to it if he knew the entire plan. He probably thought it was just a fantasy in her head. He pictured himself in bed with two women, but not like this.

"You know what? He can go to hell! I'm tired of playing the little girl. I'll enjoy the rest of my stay in this beautiful place with this massive box of heart-shaped sweets, listening to music, and drinking wine. Oh…no wine, because I have to be Al at the autograph session. I don't even know why she got me into this. Maybe she knows me better than I imagined."

Beta remembered she didn't know how to return without a car. She mentioned wanting to experience what train travel was like. She left the hotel and headed straight towards the Toledo train station. The next train would leave in 20 minutes, and there were still spots available between the Asian tourists and the Madrid executives. There was enough time to smoke a cigarette, but she didn't have any left. She saw a table at the café with five women and two men and went in their direction to ask for a cigarette. The woman with the brunette guy didn't like her asking and told Beta, "You can get a pack for four euros at the cash register." Beta laughed and accepted the cigarette and the light that the lady's husband had already offered her. Turning her back in the same way a girl in a beer commercial would've, and feeling the anger of the group of women barking behind her.

It was a cold Friday, and Beta knew that Madrid would have incredible entertainment options. Soon, she would enter the universe of people who have fans and followers, not just as someone else's character.

"I wonder if the author role suits me". Beta dreamed on the train back to Atocha.

Al jumped out of bed, thinking about doing some research for the new book at a good and discreet bookstore in Madrid. She chose one near her to avoid the risk. It was cold, and the well-known is always warmer.

Lucia and Anita had messaged her asking about the weekend and her last days in Madrid, and they planned a day off from book work and the author persona for her. They asked her to trust them and to keep Saturday night open.

She said okay, assuming nothing extraordinary could happen. Strange events already surrounded her. Even though she walked the streets wearing every coat she had packed, it still wasn't enough.

A salesman at the small bookstore offered her help with the list she had made:

"The Double" by Dostoevsky,
"Frankenstein" by Mary Shelley,
"Life is a Dream" by Calderón de la Barca,
"The Tempest" by Shakespeare,
"As I Lay Dying" by Faulkner,
"The Man Who Shot Liberty Valence" by John Ford,

"Rashomon" by Kurosawa.

"The Manchurian Candidate" by Jonathan Demme,

"The Ghost Writer" and "Zuckerman Bound" by Philip Roth.

The perfect way to start an afternoon of research and inspiration. She knew her theme wasn't anything original, and needed to see how skilled writers had approached this topic in their works. She wasn't anything more than a debut author, "with a sub-17 literacy level." Which wasn't about her age, but to her lack of baggage and stylistic experience.

Al savored her books, taking millions of notes and setting aside the most expressive pieces. Even though she was focused, she had the feeling that someone was reading over her shoulder. Holding her breath and, despite her rapidly beating heart, refusing to look at who was standing by her neck.

"*Hola,* Alberta," she heard closer than she would have liked.

She slowly turned and was surprised to see Miguel Angelo.

"*Hola,* Angelo… or Miguel?" without being able to hide her shock. "How did you find me here? I thought I was in a discreet place…"

"I went to the apartment and found this address in the laptop's search history. Be careful with technology, Alberta."

"Yeah, it's played many tricks on me," she laughed uncomfortably. "Are you alone?"

"Don't worry. Your encounter with the character will only happen around page 165 of your novel. Am I right?"

"Hahahahaha. If I could predict the steps of this book, I would say yes."

"Would you like to join me for some coffee?"

Al glanced at the pile of books and returned her gaze to Miguel, as an excuse that she couldn't just leave everything aside.

"You already ran away from me once, remember, Al?"

"Feels like a thousand years ago. So much absurdity has happened since."

"Come. I heard that someone here is a soccer fanatic. I have two seats for today's game in the press grandstand."

"At the Santiago Bernabéu??? That's a low blow! Okay, let's get this coffee."

The books could wait. Miguel Angelo was charming, but looked a lot better in his social media pictures that Alberta had stalked for hours before the bookstore. He began to develop a stomach that comes with age and more white hair than necessary. As if reading Al's thoughts, he explained that the white hairs started to appear at his temples as a sign of time, a reflection of his linguistic roots. Alberta laughed, embarrassed at her indiscretion. Had he left Beta alone? She wanted to ask, but it was best to listen to what he had to say first.

"That coffee was the beginning of one of the most incredible moments of my stay in Madrid up until then. Miguel Angelo really deserved a separate chapter. And it wasn't just because of the tickets to see the Albacete and Real Madrid play up close.

I thanked him for letting me stay at his house, and he was a little worried about Cheshire, an indolent animal, who wasn't easily fond of others. I thought he was talking about a different cat, and told him that he had kept me company, even in his bed. Miguel thought it was a lie. The power of irony is quite funny. People have been abusing it so much lately that it's become unclear whether the other person is genuinely being honest, and they don't seem to be bothered by that.

I mentioned his good literary taste and the quantity of classic Brazilian authors I found in his library, all in the original language. Then I noticed he had been speaking to me in Portuguese the entire time, almost without an accent. He confessed it was hard, but that such a beautiful language was worth the effort. I wanted to know if he will also be the translator of my first book. He smiled, already giving it away. It was already done and coming out of the printer.

I wanted to learn about his business and the branch in Barcelona, hoping he would mention his family. He dove into it unceremoniously. He had a great wife who gave him three children, despite knowing that he didn't possess the perfect fatherly characteristics. The agreement allowed him to live in Madrid during the week and spend weekends with his family, where he was a loving father and a dedicated husband. In return, he could keep his business in Madrid without much scandal from his wife. I found it all to be so modern and civilized. I couldn't understand where the ego and the pride lived within that agreement, and inevitably pictured a fictional wedding.

Then the conversation shifted to Beta, and Miguel assured me that, besides the hair, we were physically identical. I doubted it, and he mentioned something about my C-section scar. I acted as if I didn't understand what he meant, thinking it couldn't be possible. Beta told him to mention the line of birthmarks that the surgical cut had divided in half. I was mute but pissed off. "That motherfucker!" I let out a nervous laugh. He savored it with a particular cruelty. Or maybe that was just my impression? That was the most ridiculous and petulant thing I had ever heard in my life. "The scar was mine, the birthmarks too. Damn it". I hid my agitation and changed the subject.

So we talked about Carlos. Miguel found a way to ask me if we had been involved after I had separated. Why the question? – I wanted to know, taking advantage of my turn to try and torment him. "Because he speaks of you with such intimacy and affection," Miguel smiled. He had scheduled a dinner with us that night after the game, he told me. By then, it was time to go to the stadium to meet up with his friends from a sports radio station that had gotten us the tickets to the match.

Now, if you'll excuse me, I'm going to reveal an unhealthy side of me that has been asleep for quite some time. My crazy passion for soccer started precisely with the Albacete, a second division Spanish team funded by my grandfather before he migrated to Brazil. A while back (I don't remember exactly how long ago), I maintained a weekly soccer column in the most prominent newspaper of São Paulo, and followed everything that was released about the Spanish teams in the press. As I arrived near their stadium, everything hit me in full force: the expectation, the fans, the competition, and the adrenaline from the matches.

Miguel spoke on the phone with his friends from *Gestiona Radio* who would commentate on the match that afternoon. Real had already secured their spot in the EuroCopa and would only be playing this pre-scheduled friendly. All 85,000 seats were full, and outside of the stadium, you could hear the euphoria, the horns, and the anthem. Now THAT was my Y chromosome compensation!

I entered with my arm looped around Miguel's, and he was certain that I was crazy from the squeezes I gave him at each good sensation that came to my mind. Tomorrow, his wife would have to put a lot of effort into ignoring the scratch marks Beta left and the bruises on his arm caused by my childlike wonder.

I had already watched a couple of games from the press box before, but I'd say that was an orgasmic experience. As is politically correct, journalists must maintain a certain neutrality during their commentary, some self-control on the cheering, and a filter on the curse words. That was a different world. The male hormones were in prehistoric mode, amidst the smoke of 20 lit cigarettes, as it is in all of Madrid. The swearing was at an all-time high, and the crowd's excitement was palpable, even from the press. Speaking of which, swearing in Spanish was so much more liberating. The words leave our mouth heavily, like some sort of redemption. I followed the radio transmission with my three new friends, a woman among them, completely comfortable, including aesthetically, as they didn't have any commitment to be seen by the public.

It was the highlight of my trip up until then, no doubt, and I told Miguel that the experience he had provided was better than sex. He laughed and said that he had given me everything, implying that Beta and I were the same person.

We left the game sweating and happy, and went to meet up with Carlos for dinner."

Based on the quantity of words that came out from the moment that the quotation marks opened and closed, Alberta finally seemed to be regaining the first-person narrative of her book.

Beta was back in Madrid.

Today's event was happening at the *Instituto Cervantes*, very close to where the panels happened yesterday with the authors from the Literary Festival. Al was included in the young, promising international authors category.

Among the newcomers, Beta met some contemporary Spanish authors. They were charmed by the book because it went beyond the usual discussions: the industry, support, social media, blogs, literature apps, and the survival of books in the digital era, especially with the arrival of e-book piracy in Spain. The proposed debate always ended at an impasse, presenting few options or solutions for such an ample theme. A story that mixed the limits of both of these worlds brought new breath to the topic.

Beta could really use a siesta, but the young authors were extremely excited. She felt that if Al didn't finish her new book soon, others would pop up covering the same subject before she could even blink. This idea brought her a bit of melancholy. What would happen to her at the end of the book? It'd be nice if Al planned a saga with five volumes, but Beta knew there was no reason for that.

She tried to enjoy the feeling of being famous. "It's so funny meeting those who purchase our books. It's curious to imagine the reason that brings a reader to pick up a book, skim it, pay for it, choose a corner, a moment, and enjoy the words we put in the world."

She was thankful for all those people and laughed when they brought up the question of whether she was the character or the author. "We are so many things at the same time. What about you? Who are you?" Returning the question, trying not to destroy the mystery and curiosity that had been constructed the night before. At this point in the day, the video from the lecture had already accumulated 100,000 views on YouTube. Did the *virtual sex*, contrary to the effect it had on Miguel, would have excited Al?

She had a weird feeling about her being with Miguel at that very moment. Beta felt that his interest grew when he learned about her story, as if he enjoyed the privilege of being randomly thrown into that double plot. Al won his sympathy and curiosity. Beta didn't think he would leave before she woke up, but she also hated goodbyes. It was better that way anyway, without much drama, and that was the agreement from the beginning.

Yes, Alberta and Miguel were together like a poorly tuned walkie-talkie full of static. Beta swore she could hear another station in her head. Or was it the swarm of tablets, phones, and thousands of devices that were interfering with the most sensitive brains?

No. No, it wasn't just a feeling. Beta distanced herself a bit from the buzz as if searching for a signal or the fine synchrony of the sound waves of an imaginary radio. At a particular moment, her slow steps stopped to hear better what was now clearly a transmission of the Real Madrid game that was happening exactly in that moment at the Santiago Bernabéu.

Beta couldn’t help but smile. Miguel probably dragged Al to the sport that touched her heart. That was the only explanation for her absence from the event. It was strange for Beta to realize she was internally rooting for Al. And her author's surrender was a surprise and a reward.

She returned to the group and extended her evening as the festival offered a closing party with jazz and an open bar. Her new friends wanted to go for a walk and breathe some fresh, non-literary Madrid air before coming back for the next commitment their editors forced them to attend.

Beta ran away with them for a bit, and on the street, many cars crossed her path with happy fans singing the Real Madrid anthem. Al and Miguel could be found in one of them, making their way towards a business dinner with Carlos.

“Business dinner? I hope that's not all it is.” She maliciously smiled, wishing she could be the author of that story to make sure Al had a memorable night.

The traffic outside the stadium was terrible.

"Miguel said we would walk to *Tommy Mel's* to meet up with Carlos, only five blocks away from the stadium. I was impressed to find out that it was 53°F and I wasn't cold. The feeling of watching my team play against Real Madrid in the world's best stadium was priceless. How incredible it was to feel alive! I then realized it had been a long time since I had used an exclamation point."

Speaking of punctuation, Al had forgotten entirely about Beta and her afternoon of autographs. It honestly didn't seem like the right time for them to meet up yet, she remembered, as she thanked Miguel 50,000 times for the fantastic game they had just watched. She offered to pay for dinner in retribution, knowing that most of the Spanish rich men would be traditionalist enough to refuse.

The restaurant was more of a diner with typical 1950s American décor, which surprised Alberta, who had expected a more formal place suitable for deals and business. But who said work and fun had to walk so separately?

They found Carlos alone at a table between the noisy fans, evidently tired from his last-minute trip. "He immediately saw us when we entered, first with a smile that he tried to hide, then turning into a strange face, masking a sentiment that is difficult to detect so quickly. Jealousy? Unlikely."

Alberta greeted her friend with a hug, a little more excitedly than usual, still due to the match. If she had stayed a bit longer, she would have been trading her Real shirt, which she had just won from the press team, with other fans. "Breathe in the cold air, Al, and try to get back to normal", she recommended to herself. Carlos also noticed the unusual break in character and extra affection, making an ironic comment to Miguel (whom he had called Angelo before learning that, to his friends, he was known as Miguel), asking how he managed to put me in such a good mood in so little time. The Spanish editor smiled, letting the mystery linger in the air. "Men, tsk, tsk. When they're not competing on the field, they're competing in life."

"I threw my bag next to Miguel and chose to sit next to Carlos. It seemed more sensible and professional as we would be negotiating together with Miguel, before listening to the other two proposals from the competing publishers the following day.

It was challenging to switch the conversation to business. The atmosphere was too relaxed, as a huge soccer game had just taken place, and to top it all off, a couple was covering Marilyn and Elvis performing at the restaurant, making the ambiance even more lively.

Their presence was the starting point for the topic of my new book. First, the two began discussing the idea and its implications while evaluating the chaos I was creating. They were betting on my ability to get out of it, throwing out possible endings to the story, citing classic references, and engaging in a typical nerd conversation that was capable of inflating my ego and camouflaging the astronomical quantity of alcohol we had consumed.

We started with margaritas to toast and warm up the body from the cold, and didn't stop drinking tequila. Thank goodness for the greasy food from the restaurant, which helped us tolerate the drinks. None of us seemed too worried about the percentage of alcohol in our bloodstreams. It was Friday, Real had scored some goals, and the night was *una niña*. I caught myself speaking terrible Spanish, a courage that only appeared when I started to get drunk.

Miguel swore that Beta existed. He told Carlos that one day they would discover they had been tricked by twins. Carlos, who has known me for 20 years, claimed that maybe we had been separated at birth. Miguel laughed and apologized, explaining that he didn't have much time to learn more about my twin. 'Intellectually speaking', he stressed, putting himself in an even more complicated position and earning laughs from our side of the table. He said he would love to be present at the climactic meeting in the book, but had to return to Barcelona today right after dinner. We were relieved when we found out he would take the train, because in this state, he wouldn't even be able to start the car.

Carlos shared a bit about the repercussions the panel had gotten, which he thought I wasn't going to show up to, from the Brazilian media. I ended up on the trending topics on Twitter, capturing the attention of readers beyond the genres that were naturally suited to me. 'And that's a good thing?' Carlos laughed at my question. The annoying implications I have been complaining about recently seemed foolish compared to what life had offered me.

I noticed that my body was very close to Carlos's. Perhaps due to the cold, or perhaps deep down, I missed him. There you go. The drinks were already putting me in that mushy phase of 'I love you, Carlos. You're such a great friend.' Unintentionally, I had disconnected from the conversation that the other two were maintaining between themselves, and I reflected on the role that Carlos plays in my life.

We met in college, and initially, we had a friendly rivalry. He was the one who introduced me to João, since he was always more connected than I was. He soon revealed himself to be an exceptional columnist and went on to open his own publishing company, which today ranks among the top five publishers in Brazil. Since then, we have always run into each other. Julia has a genuine adoration for him, as he was a key figure in my post-separation phase when he agreed to publish my book. Our friendship was always very flippant. There was no room for anything to happen between us: no wild sex or a friends-with-benefits situation. To be honest, I never saw Carlos with anyone. Either because I never paid attention or because I thought he was gay, the discreet kind. And yet, there I was. With my guard down, enjoying human connection, and almost lying down on his arm.

I opened my eyes in the middle of my thoughts, and he looked at me very seriously and very close. I looked at him, too, in a moment that seemed to last for an eternity. A silent conversation that had been postponed for years. Was I understanding what he wanted to say, but didn't? Or was I just lonely and traveling? I decided to put an end to that by quickly making a face and masking the tension.

I think Miguel soon caught on to what we hadn't even noticed. He looked at his watch, organized his things, and jokingly hummed a part of a famous Brazilian song about missing the train home. We fell into laughter as we stood up to say goodbye. It was quite a difficult task since the rounds of margaritas had surpassed our common-sense limit. Miguel hugged me and asked me to leave the key to his apartment with the housekeeper on Monday, as I thanked him again and again. This time, more sluggishly and nasally. He advised that I not be too hard on Beta, who, according to him, was the coolest and most dangerous woman he had met recently. "Dangerous?" I asked. He pointed dramatically to his heart and, with that, turned his back and disappeared in a taxi towards the station.

We decided to close the bill, and I felt confused just thinking about going home. Would I even know how to get there? I asked Carlos to put me in a taxi or take me to bed, and laughed at my courage. A second later, I wanted to take back what I had said, but it was too late. He was silent as we walked out, drunk with our arms wrapped around each other. The tequila was still in effect in a way that every idea we had seemed original. That man next to me was the most real thing that I had around there. Carlos brought me feelings of familiarity, trustworthiness, and safety. I felt a deep sense of gratitude and affection for him. So much history, so many jokes, and ups and downs. It didn't make sense for me to want to sleep with him like this, so randomly. But I wasn't in the best state to evaluate all of that. Or was that maybe the best state? Whose point of view is it from anyway?

And reality intervened.

'Wake up, Al. We arrived,' Carlos said in the taxi.

We walked into his hotel with our arms linked, without saying a word. He gave me a real hug in the elevator, and I felt that he meant something more with that. He gently started kissing my neck, which woke me up yet threw me into a weird trance that brought up a deep suffering I fought not to access anymore. It was both good and not at the same time. Too intense. It wasn't a stranger kissing me. What he lived resonated within me, and this rift we accidentally opened in this moment connected with something I had hidden from an encounter predicted years ago. Sober me would've run away as fast as possible. Drunk me was having a tougher time. I tried to enjoy the situation without rationalizing everything.

In the room, I went to the bathroom to take a look in the mirror, and my reflection was frightening. The euphoria of the soccer game had passed, and the one from the drinks was rapidly fading. It was best to beat the clock and do whatever we had to do before the old and tired Alberta took back the reins. But what do we have to do? I opened the bathroom door to find a visibly tired Carlos, with no intention of abandoning the unexpected chance that appeared in front of him. Take it, Carlos. 'Cause it's yours.

As he kissed me, I wondered if he also questioned the meaning of that moment. It felt good. The rhythm seemed slower than usual, probably due to the alcoholic circumstances of both people involved, but he was good at the preliminaries. I also didn't want to have my performance evaluated that night because I was acutely aware that I wasn't fully present. To the point where I felt like I had shut down in between moments, losing a bit of the logical sequence of things. Did I doze off?

I was walking a fine line, where people often can't remember what they did the night before when they wake up the next day, which was a shame. I wanted to have crossed that line, and truly not remembered what had happened, because it didn't happen.

Looking back now, it wasn't a dream. Carlos tried to concentrate and overcome the preliminaries, but the tequila was a killer when it came to numbing the extremities. I didn't have the strength to come up with any motivating tricks, so we ended up giving up on what we already knew wouldn't happen.

In fiction, the scene would cut immediately to the next sunny day, where everything went back to normal. The subject would become a joke, and the story would continue without any mishaps. But the only certainty that I had in that moment, even drunk, was that we were real.

Nothing was said. We hugged each other and cuddled into a slightly awkward spoon, and in 40 seconds, I noticed that Carlos had fallen into a deep sleep. Unfortunately, I could never fall asleep that easily. I hoped he had managed to cross the threshold of amnesia. One less person to question everything and to deal with the frustration.

Sliding on my clothes, I tripped around the room, eventually making my way into a taxi to take me home, where I am now, without a single ounce of sleepiness in my body."

Day Eight

Saturday dawned cloudy and with a light drizzle.

Beta was beautiful, light, and free throughout the *Museo Reina Sofia's* corridors. Her hair was impeccable, without a drop of rain in it. She walked through the empty corridors, despite being someone who had spent the previous day packed with appointments and contacts.

She encountered a louder buzz in one of the rooms and saw the incredible *Guernica*, Picasso's most famous painting, and considered an icon of the Spanish Civil War. Large in size and expressiveness, the piece reported the German bombing on April 26, 1937, suffered by the small Spanish town, which the piece is named after. Beta curiously watched the documentary about the damage the tragedy left behind. She read about the painters' work and became interested in its repercussions until she found an interesting fact online.

At the end of the Second World War, historical revisionists couldn't find proof that the Germans were to blame for the destruction of the city, attributing the act to the Spanish Republicans who were retreating and had exploded their existing arsenal. *The Great Guernica Fraud* is the title of the study published in 1973 by the National Review, which revealed that Picasso had finished the painting before the bombing even happened. His original theme was the barbarity behind bullfighting, and its previous title was *La Muerte del Torero Joselito.* Beta laughed while recognizing the painter's shamelessness in tricking the world and self-promoting.

Because it was her nature to find a correlation to everything in her life, Beta thought it was a good time to pay a bit more attention to her relationship with Alberta. She wondered who she could share her plans with.

Checking her phone, she found a *Hola* from Miguel. She smiled maliciously, already predicting the entire conversation, and hesitated for a few minutes before proceeding. She loved turning a period into a comma. She opened up her phone and started typing.

"*Eres loco*, Miguel? ;-)"

"*Sí, por ti, Beta.* :-P"

"Hahahaha. You were able to mislead three children and a woman?"

"They're at the movie theater, and I came to a coffee shop to negotiate with my favorite writer."

"You know very well I'm just a character."

"That's why I'm calling. To tell you, I think you're Alberta's best character."

"*Gracias, cariño.* You're very special too. Sadly, you're real."

"I didn't want to run away from Toledo, but I had to process our night together from a distance."

"I figured. And have you come to a 'conclusion'?"

"No, haha. I just know it was good."

"See? There's never anything beyond what we feel. Either it's good or it's not. Simple."

"I can't have such a simple outlook on things. Which is sad because it's a lot less fun. I also had to come back to reality. :-("

"And take Al out to live a little…"

"Hmmm, so you already know?"

"I just know you went to the game. Is there anything else to know? I doubt it, haha."

"That was all. But it was incredible. She is incredible".

"No wonder she created such an amazing, unbelievable character like me! Lol"

"True. Where are you?"

"Now? In front of a Picasso…"

"Already? I barely turned my back!"

"A huge Picasso, hahahahaha."

"I bet it's the *Guernica.*"

"*Sí, sí. Reina Sofia.*"

"Well, I can't compete with that. No one can. But I wish I were with you."

The conversation always went back to where it started. What a predictable script. Playing with fire sometimes burns your fingers.

"So you went home at the right time ;)"

"I know. Dumb of me to fall in love with a character, right?"

"You just think you are. Soon you're going to miss someone else, haha."

"I hope so. And this someone else can't be you?"

"AI decides that. But I think it's very unlikely."

Beta threw the bait, pretending to be uninterested.

"I thought you had an escape plan at the end of the book, Beta."

"I don't know if I'm that smart. Fiction has its limits, lol."

"I can think of something. At the end of the day, publishers are frustrated authors, hahaha."

"Forget it, Miguel. Why drag this out?"

"Because it's good. And you said it yourself, that's always the only reason."

"True. :D"

"I thought about keeping Al here for a couple more weeks. I offered an irrefusable contract, but Carlos will meet with two other publishers today. I hope he gives me the chance to make a counteroffer for the new book."

"You don't know how to lose, do you?"

"And you have a lot to gain with that."

"Other than your little puns? lol… Maybe we've already experienced everything."

"I'm typically a little insatiable. I thought we had that in common."

"Pull your strings. I would love for Al to accept that ;)"

"I'll let you know! *Te quiero! Mucho*. Got to go."

"*Te quiero*! <3"

And the app said he was offline.

Beta imagined herself again in Miguel's apartment, listening to more stories, living new experiences, and discovering special places. This time, she would enter the scene fully armed. After all, this story needed some spice, conflict, and competition. She began to grasp the significance of expectation in the lives of real people. She could be more than a planned character. She could use the fact that many were confusing her with the author to her advantage.

Morning arrived, and Alberta wanted to bottle up the euphoria of the day before, but the evening's events were burned into her memory. Something had been taken out of place, bothering her a bit. Like an itch that left her restless, Al decided to lose her mind at a famous hair salon in the city. It came as a recommendation from her highly connected friend, Anita. She needed a change, and that meant new hair.

In the waiting room, she began to stress about the comments written in the literary section of the Spanish journal about her career and her new book. Critics questioned her cultural baggage and the likelihood of the story. Some thought Al was pushing it too far, and it was all a huge publicity stunt involving her writer friends. Others felt that her infamous bad mood had turned into a persecution complex. Psychologists all over social media evaluated her appearance, rummaged through her past, and her first book. There was even a fake Twitter account called "schizophrenic writer". Everything culminated in a giant circus that gave her professional repercussions and a huge headache.

Her mom had already shared her worries early in the morning, ignoring the time zone difference and asking her to come back using a little bit of emotional manipulation through Julia, who refused to speak to her mother on the phone. Thanks to technology, her reputation as a crazy lady must have arrived in São Paulo. This is what a real bad hair day looked like.

She took her seat in the salon, grateful for all the hair dryer noise, gossip, and vanity that represented the worst parts of the real world. After snorting and cursing herself for starting the whole story, she decided it was time to change many things in her life. Starting with her hair. She asked them to bleach her locks to the whitest blonde that the bleach could provide. She had to reinforce her request several times, a clear sign that the hairdresser thought it would come out terribly. But Al was secure in what she wanted: to look different than herself, Beta, and every other person in the world.

Laptop in hand and a head burning from the chemicals, Al emailed everyone she knew, as if the world would end tomorrow. She needed to reconnect with reality and get her feet on the ground. She needed her childhood friends, her therapist, her mom, her daughter, her friends from the newspaper where she abandoned her soccer column, and the people from the magazine. She desperately needed to reconnect with her ties, untangle the most beautiful and firm ones, stretch out the ends, and hold on to them very tightly so she wouldn't lose them again.

Her phone pinged with a new message from Carlos. Alberta put the device on her lap and, in slow motion, with the caution one would use to avoid detonating a bomb. She looked at her iPhone, lacking the courage to check the contents of the message. She knew words had the power to change someone's life. Words often burned more than that yellow goo on her head. It wasn't a coincidence that the word spell could refer to naming letters aloud or a magical charm.

"If it were work-related, he would have called. I'm going to pretend that I don't have service, or that my battery died, I don't know." Al didn't want to analyze the meaning at that moment. She needed to reflect on how she wanted to deal with the implications that last night could cause. Strategies needed to be elaborated in case Carlos remembered everything, if he remembered some of it, and if he forgot absolutely everything and deleted it all from his mind. She fervently rooted for that last one. The best thing to do is turn off her phone.

Another app opened on her laptop screen, bringing her Spanish friends online and asking about the preparations for the party tonight. Al still had to find a costume. They had already chosen theirs. Anita would be dressed as Wilma from The Flintstones, and Lucia would be Lucy from Peanuts. "In this cold, girls? You guys are completely crazy." Al had thought about dressing as a bullfighter or a flamenco dancer, and couldn't decide which one she would feel more ridiculous in. They all laughed, and Alberta found this virtual conversation to be the perfect distraction to forget Carlos' unread message.

Would she finally meet Beta tonight? She could no longer remember which page of the book they were on after the omniscient narrator took the story from her. She felt a weird calm and sensed that Beta was probably more dangerous than she seemed.

Beta decided to rent the costumes for the party they would attend that night. She tried to warn Al, but she seemed unreachable.

The costume store was huge, and Beta started looking for a pair that made sense. There were large racks of clothing with modest costumes, and others not so much. Many people crowded the fitting rooms. The *Gabana* party stirred up the city.

She couldn't wait to finally go to the most *privé* nightclub in Madrid.

She stopped in front of the Blue Fairy's dress and Pinocchio's outfit. "Al would be the fairy godmother who gave me life. No, that's a touchy subject. I like the Peter Pan one. I'll be the girl who doesn't want to grow up, but I think this Tinkerbell dress is too short for her." She walked further and loved the Alice and the Mad Hatter, but truly lost it at the Avatar costume. A super sexy blue jumpsuit, and a long braided black wig. She doubted Al would ever agree to painting her face blue. It was getting difficult. She walked along, lost amidst all the racks in the couple's costumes section. Hansel and Gretel, Wonder Twins, Smurfs, Charlie Brown and Lucy, Batman and Robin, ketchup and mustard, The Little Prince and the Fox, good cop and bad cop.

Nothing truly caught her eye. She went back to Avatar. They needed to be identical if Beta wanted to follow through with the plan she came up with that morning. But that blue lycra suit didn't match with her author. From afar, she saw a pair of overalls left behind in the fitting room and walked over to see what costume it was. Her eyes sparkled. Finally, she found what was needed: a pair of jean overalls from the video game characters, Mario and Luigi. Simple, basic, and warmer than other costumes. She checked the size and decided to rent the red and green shirts, as well as the hats with their initials, to differentiate them.

It was perfect because it would hide their bodies and camouflage their hair. Even better, it included two mustaches to complete the fake androgynous look they both loved. Beta was satisfied.

Al wouldn't have much time to complain or look for another costume. The past was already knocking on her door.

Alberta was radiant with her new look. She would now have to deal with the paleness her new icy blond hair brought to her skin. But the stock of makeup she had purchased was sufficient for that. Amid these thoughts, she opened the door to Miguel's apartment and almost fell back.

"João?"

"Carlos and I have been calling you for hours, damn it. Can I come in? "

Instinctively, Al touched his arm to see if it was actually him in flesh and blood. There was an awkward moment about how they should greet each other. He offered his face, and she stood there with no reaction. There had to be a plausible explanation.

"You look different. What a change of hair! "João said, evaluating the apartment.

"My hair? What color do you see? "

"What do you mean? Do you not know?" He laughed, throwing her a curious look.

"Never mind," she said. She was starting to come off as truly crazy.

"I'm here with the band to play a concert in Berlin. I had a connecting flight here and decided to stop by to see you. But it took me two hours to find you throughout the city."

"A friend of mine loaned me this apartment. Did I invite you?"

"No… Did you?"

She was a little embarrassed by the question. It seemed like she was saying he showed up uninvited when Al just wanted to make it seem like she was having "tech issues". She can't remember if she said that aloud or in thought.

"I missed you. I think I wanted a hug," João said lowly, bringing back a tone that they hadn't used with each other in a long time. Alberta was shocked.

"You came all the way over here for a hug?" She said, immediately regretting her lack of sensibility.

"Of course not, Berta. Don't make things difficult…"

"Why did you call me Berta?" The question rose with her annoyance.

"I don't know. Because Julia calls you that sometimes. Hey, relax."

Al took a deep breath and apologized. Ever since she was little, her daughter had been calling her by that name and making up random nicknames. It was best to grab two beers in the kitchen so they could relax. On the way, she tried to explain herself without looking at João.

"Forget it. I have been having problems with the character I created."

"I've heard the rumors…"

She looked out of the kitchen and saw her ex-husband sitting on Miguel's couch.

"You did? So the gossip has reached the "rock world"?"

"Yeah…" He said, smiling and thanking her for the beer. "But everyone knows how your head gets stuck in the clouds when you're involved in your writing. You're in your own little 'literary world'. Cheers!" He completed, lifting his can.

"Some things never change, huh?" Al smiled ironically, returning the toast. João had an incredible ability to bring out the worst in her. She didn't have to always be on the defensive, feel cornered, and cheated simultaneously. She was sitting before the man she had chosen to marry and to father her child.

"It's strange, Al, but I've wanted to do things differently."

"Like what?"

"I don't know. Like drag you to Germany with me, for example?"

Before she could even demonstrate surprise, Al fired off:

"Your fans weren't available?"

"See? Are you capable of having a conversation without poking me?"

There. It happened again.

Al sighed, recognizing:

"I try, but it's almost automatic. I don't think I believe in anything you say anymore. What can I do?" She smiled, trying to apologize.

"Okay. I know I'm confused, but this trip could be a new starting point for us."

"João, you say that as if it's going to be a super honeymoon, and we both know it won't be. It's YOUR band and YOUR concert, and rehearsal, and sound check, and meetings, and sponsored events."

"You can check out the city while I do all that."

"Leave my story behind so I can wander around Berlin alone?"

"That could become another book, right?"

"I think after this one, I'm hanging up my boots."

"Come on, come with me."

Al thought she wanted to hear that. They were the right words said at the wrong time. She pretended to consider the proposal, but it was a lie. Maybe she had already gotten used to being alone. Or perhaps she was incapable of erasing a period.

"Honestly, João, I have deeply desired a proposal, an invite, or a chance. But right now it doesn't make any sense. We've already lived our best moments. What I miss are those times, not us together. Do you understand?"

"On one end, I thought that, too. On the other hand, I thought we deserved another chance. That was dumb of me."

"It's not dumb. Maybe today I'm just a different person," she said, straightening the ends of her new hair as if the bleach had deep transformational powers.

"Julia would love it if we figured things out, right?"

"I think so."

"But it's not gonna happen…"

"I don't think so."

"Okay. I couldn't die without asking."

"Come here," she gave him the hug he sought. It was a bit colder than she expected. A clear signal that he had already closed himself off, too.

"So that's it," he tried to sum it up. "We like each other, we'll support each other from afar, but we don't know how to be together anymore. That's kind of sad."

"Perfect lives only exist in fairy tales, right?"

"That's true. I'm going to go now. Carlos is waiting for me outside."

"Really? Why didn't he come up with you?"

"I must have seemed very confident with my reconciliation plans." He smiled charmingly, a little embarrassed. "He didn't want to get in the way".

"Carlos is incredible," Al said unintentionally.

"He just said the same thing about you. I think he's always been in love with you."

"Red flag", Alberta thought, wanting to know what else he could have told João, but also not wanting to. Carlos was discreet, she remembered.

"Come on, João. That's all on your head."

"No, it's not. Now that you don't want me anymore, you can try Carlos. We're basically brothers, we're both rooting for you…"

"Isn't it a bit soon for you to try to push me onto someone else?"

"Just trying to break the ice."

"I've actually been quite tired of people who are so similar to others."

"Like in your book. I hope you finish it soon. Well, I have to go."

"Have a good trip. Break a leg," She tried to ease the tension.

João made a face as he entered the elevator and disappeared.

What just happened? Julia would definitely revolt against her now because she didn't take her dad back. Al knew it wouldn't be long before João told his daughter his plan had failed.

She closed the door and heard steps in the hallway. Thinking that João had forgotten something, she unintentionally opened the door, just in time to notice a figure entering the elevator. It smelled like good perfume. "Hmmmm, my perfume!" She tripped on a bag that sat on the welcome mat with a note attached:

"There must be praised, some certainty, if not of loving well, then not." Dylan Thomas and Beta. See you later, my dear author.

By mere seconds, she didn't run into Beta, who left her costume for the party at the door. Had she listened to the entire conversation?

Al stood in front of the mirror, feeling ridiculous. "Relax, everyone's going to embarrass themselves. At least I'm hidden and warm below this jumpsuit," trying to console herself.

The taxi driver greeted her "sir" thanks to the mustache and hat. There wasn't a less sexy costume in the world. She started to worry again about Beta's interference in her life. "At least she didn't choose a slutty costume." She decided to play the game and gave the taxi driver the address in a deeper voice. The heavy overcoat she wore wasn't helping at all. The party started late, and she tried to nap to stay up until a reasonable time. Instead of resting, she kept thinking about João, Carlos, and Miguel— so many men to deal with in such little time.

The *Gabana Club* was the most famous dance club in the city. Famous among celebrities, surrounded by scary-looking security guards at the door, and commanded by a hostess who determined who got in and who didn't, without any criteria. It was way too cold to stand outside, waiting for their goodwill to let them in, she complained in thought as she got out of the taxi. But her friends were awaiting her in their summer outfits below their coats that draped down to their feet. It was incredible how people there gained a higher tolerance for lower temperatures. She thought of the prostitutes who spent the night at the *Gran Via* in boots and miniskirts. On the day she spoke to them, some men walked by asking them to lift their shirts to see their goose-bumped breasts.

Lucia and Anita burst out laughing when they saw Al dressed as Luigi. They were already a bit tipsy and accompanied by three friends they had pregamed with. Al felt she was about four doses behind them. They descended the stairs and squeezed into the coat room. She knew many places like that in São Paulo: good music, expensive drinks, snobby and beautiful people. The environment was cool, but Al doubted she would attract anyone's attention in that jumpsuit-baseball-cap-mustache outfit. It seemed like Beta wanted to keep all the sexual experiences to herself. All that was left for Alberta was exes and whiskey dicks. Best not to think about that now.

Alberta's shirt was green. Assuming Beta would be dressed exactly like her, except in a red shirt, she started searching for someone like that in the club. Whenever someone in a red shirt walked by, Al's heart started beating rapidly, thinking it was time for the meet-up. But the place was already packed, and Alberta decided to drink a bit to get her mind off things, giving in to the blue atmosphere the space had. There was a buzz that the Real Madrid team and Cristiano Ronaldo were coming, which made Al give up on looking for Beta. Instead, she searched for a second dose, and the bartender laughed, saying she had just served her Mario Bros friend. Beta was there, and soon they would find each other. She shared with her friends her expectation of meeting up with her character for the first time, and they said they would also like to see it to believe if Beta truly existed.

It was time to confront the massive line at the female bathroom. Lucia was in a lively conversation with Santiago, the friend dressed as a cop, and the owner of the house where they had pregamed. Suddenly, she stopped speaking, poked Anita, and pointed to a dark corner of the VIP area. A weird couple was making out, Superman and Mario? No. It was Beta! The two started screaming with happiness, and from afar, they noticed she looked very similar to Al. Not similar. It was practically Alberta in a red shirt. "Was Al playing a trick on them? I'll only believe Beta actually exists if she stands side by side with Al!" They agreed on that. They needed to find their friend in the bathroom quickly, but decided to wait for her there. From the intensity of the kiss, that couple would not be leaving that area anytime soon.

Al took a long time to return, and obviously, the couple was no longer in sight. Alberta had run into the people from the radio who had taken her to the game. It took them a while to recognize her, but they had also seen Beta in the club and found her appearance very familiar, even below the hat and mustache. Al tried to explain the reality vs. fiction partnership, but the music and the cheers were too loud. They asked about Miguel, and Al quickly changed the subject. It would be difficult to convince the group then that nothing had happened between them, just between him and Beta.

His friends looked silly dressed as The Avengers, and they told her she wasn't the only one with a doppelganger. As is customary in the celebrity world, Cristiano Ronaldo sent a look-alike to the club to discreetly take pictures in the VIP area, create a stir, and then leave quickly. Alberta couldn't hide her disappointment. Maybe no one could stand playing the role of themselves anymore.

Third drink in, and Al started dancing with Pedro, Mr. Incredible, a friend of the girl's who is much younger than her. A model with an angel face and almost nothing in his head. If she wanted to have a fling with a Spanish man, the opportunity was dancing right in front of her. She kissed Pedro briefly, saying she would return soon, but needed to go to the bathroom again. He was no longer in sight when she returned, and Al cursed herself for one more missed opportunity. "What could I do? I have a small bladder," Her friends joked that Beta, her character, who was a lot smarter than her, had run away with Pedro.

The bartender joked about her twin sister, and Al was already losing count of the number of vodka and energy drinks she was on. Pedro returned, saying they should leave the club and head to his house, asking Al why she kept switching shirts all the time. "It must be hard being two people at once," he laughed, kissing her neck. Alberta didn't understand the joke and wanted to know more. "You just jumped me as you left the men's bathroom! Might be time to stop drinking, beautiful."

Beta was taking advantage of their similarity to plant suspicion in other people's minds. Al needed to find her soon.

Her Mr. Incredible took a paper napkin from his pocket and gave it to Al.

"You told me not to read it and to give it to you when I saw you again with the green shirt. Here you go."

Al opened the note as she pushed Pedro away. Suddenly, she wasn't interested in him anymore. "Find me in the bathroom in the second stall from the left. Bring a friend."

Understanding that Beta would undo the farce and wanting a witness, she called Lucia and had to persist to pull her away from Santiago. She didn't know what time it was exactly, but knew that in the club, it was "no one belongs to anyone" time. Two minutes of distraction, and Mr. Incredible Pedro was already whispering in Catwoman's ear.

Lucia reluctantly followed Al, saying she was ruining her chances of sleeping with a cop. Alberta was happy because there was no longer a line for the bathroom. "Please, please, I need someone to see that she is real," Al implored.

They soon realized the stall was closed. Fighting for space in the mirror, there was a fortune teller, a Pocahontas, a Cinderella, two sexy nurses, and a Wonder Woman. "*Es una chica*!" Lucia told them, as they thought it was weird to see someone in there with a mustache, and dressed like a man.

Al looked below the stall and didn't see anyone's feet. They called Beta while they pushed the door, which was just ajar. All they found was a red shirt taken off quickly, and a hat with an embroidered M lying on top of the toilet. Has Beta evaporated? Alberta couldn't take that reversal of expectations anymore. She started to get really pissed off.

Lucia took her friend by the arm, saying she was being too neurotic with that whole story. Deep down, she wanted to say they wondered if Al had made it all up, but felt bad for her friend. They were there to relax, have fun, and forget about the book, weren't they? Alberta apologized, but her brain was going a mile a minute trying to understand it all.

Had Beta enjoyed the role of author so much that she thought she could transform herself into one? It was time to go home. Things were getting too confusing.

Day Nine

It was past two in the afternoon on Sunday. Anita and Lucia enjoyed their hangover below immense dark sunglasses in a bohemian corner of the city. They talked about Alberta as they waited for her, who, as usual, was late. They had been worried about this whole character thing and were questioning what could truly be happening.

From Lucia's standpoint, as a psychologist, she hadn't worried at first. But she thought Al's behavior in Spain had been strange. She exchanged messages with Al's mom asking about her friend's extreme thinness. Her mom informed her that maybe it was the result of hyperthyroidism that a recent blood test revealed. Al never followed up with a doctor about it. Lucia said the disease left the person affected extremely agitated, out of breath, irritated, and confused. And what about the cat Al spoke of so often? She confessed that sometimes she felt like they were in Alice in Wonderland. But Lucia thought it was best to avoid that topic, as that book and its author were so insane that medicine had at least three syndromes inspired by the piece, including the White Rabbit Syndrome for people who constantly have issues with time.

Being more pragmatic, Anita bet that it was all a stunt for the launch of her new book. Al used literature to fill a giant hole within herself, and she became obsessed with this universe, success, and the virtual followers. She couldn't have a minute of peace without being called by someone on her phone, and she didn't seem so tired and hopeless about life. They speculated about Beta. That person didn't make sense.

The common opinion was that this character was a huge farce from Alberta's part. Starting with the encounter with

Miguel. Anita remembered when they had lunch together at the Prado Museum, and towards the end, her friend asked to be called Beta when they scheduled the date with Miguel. She chose to meet him, and it seemed as if she knew what she was doing. Maybe she hid behind the nickname so she could make up the whole story without feeling the guilt of kissing a married man. The author and the character were the perfect alibis for one another.

Alberta arrived agitated and quickly stated they were prohibited from speaking about the book, characters, Beta, or Miguel. She hadn't slept at all from all the thinking she was doing and had given up. She would finish the book that day and fly back home the following morning.

“Let's enjoy this sunny Sunday and buy things we don't need.”

Lucia and Anita made Al sit at the bar to eat. Unwillingly, she accepted a small tapa and left it half eaten, lying that she had just had breakfast. Her friends looked at each other and decided to question Al about her thinness. Alberta confessed that she hadn’t been feeling well and almost passed out at the *El Corte Inglés* store on Thursday when she went Christmas shopping. Lucia asked if she had insomnia, palpitations, irritation, and mental confusion. She received a large laugh from Al, wondering if anyone could say they didn't feel one of those things nowadays.

“I know you want to take care of me, darling, but there’s genuinely nothing wrong with me.”

They knew Alberta hated going to the doctor and believed that shiatsu and acupuncture cured everything in life.

They insisted on wanting to know how long it had been since Al had gone in for a physical.

"Oh, I bet my mom has spewed her drama at you. Having a hypochondriac family is not easy! She thinks I have some sort of thyroid alteration."

"And you don't?"

"I think I have a high T3 level. But a friend looked at the bloodwork and said I shouldn't worry about it."

"A doctor friend?"

"No…" Alberta smiled, dismantling her lie.

"Alberta!" Her friends exclaimed reprimanding. Al smiled and changed the subject, promising to redo the tests as soon as she returned from her trip.

"Now, enough of that, I don't want to waste another minute of my last day in Madrid. Time to see *El Rastro*!" She excitedly declared, chugging her last bit of wine and waving at the waiter for their bill.

They found Alberta's sudden excitement strange. It seemed more like an agitation moved by repressed anger. Still, they decided to listen to their friend and tranquilly walk along the stands of the wonderful flea market in the city on Sundays. They spent a lot of time trying on hats from a large old lady with extremely long nail extensions, and getting goosebumps each time she offered them a new style. Despite their nausea, they couldn't stop asking for hats and speaking lowly in Portuguese about all the disgusting microscopic beings, existent and non-existent, that lived below those nails. Mold, mildew, cryptococcus, esquistossomo, Entamoeba. They giggled until the lady couldn't take it anymore and kicked them out.

Between vintage furniture that Al loved, but couldn't fit in her luggage, she ended up haggling and buying an old vanity mirror, and imagined how she could imprison Beta inside it.

Al pushed the door to Miguel's apartment with her body. Her arms were covered in bags. Other than the mirror, she also bought a vintage edition of *Don Quixote*, three scarves, and a beautiful engraving by *Joaquim Sorolla* called *Chicos en la Playa*, which she didn't have time to see the original at the Prado up close. On her last day, she regretted not embarking towards Spain on her original date. She was going home without visiting museums or seeing any stores, and buying a thousand new pens and Moleskines.

Cheshire came to greet her with a long meow. “I'm going to miss you too, sweetheart,” she said out loud, trying to pick him up unsuccessfully. His fur bristled, and Al had never heard him meow that much. Throwing her body on the couch, she took off her boots and thought about packing her bags for the following day. She loved flying during the day on her way home from the few international trips she had taken. The time could be used to reminisce on what she experienced, write down her impressions, and calculate her credit card bill. Deciding to write a bit before taking a scorching hot shower, she started looking for her laptop in the living room. She tried to remember if it had been moved and looked at the outlet, but only saw the extension plugged in.

She jumped as the cat wouldn't stop meowing from Miguel's room. Already feeling something was wrong, Al slowly made her way over. On top of the bed was a colorful Russian doll that she picked up and started to open. Other identical ones appeared until the smallest one popped up, wrapped in a small note written in her handwriting. Or theirs?

"You're not doing so great. Let me take care of our story. Beta"

The certainty that her laptop had been stolen made Al run towards her suitcase in search of the flash drive, which she had a (now the only) backup copy of her book. Relief filled her body as she saw it was still hidden. Running to Miguel's computer to verify the contents, she realized the last five chapters of the book were not saved, "Shit, shit, shit!"

Al wanted to leave that place. She called Carlos and spoke so rapidly that he might've only understood the part about his hotel's address. After throwing everything in her suitcase, which didn't close anymore because of the recent purchases, she sat on top of it, jumped, and heard the zipper screaming in effort. *Listo*!

In the bathroom, everything was left behind, rounding out roughly 50 mini products she had purchased, including things her family and friends had asked her to bring back. She searched for a large bag, recalling that all of them had been thrown into the office trash can. While dodging Cheshire, who was fighting with a ball of yarn, she found a sturdy bag but stopped upon seeing her first novel lying on a pile of papers on the desk. She opened the copy and found many annotations (from Miguel?) in the corners of the page, highlighted passages, and post-its marking excerpts. Al couldn't understand the handwriting, but thought it was best to bring it with her. It was weird to think about someone reading her book. What was actually weird was agreeing to stay at a stranger's house. To her luck, he wasn't a psychopath.

She tripped again on her way out of the room and felt something below her feet. In a couple of minutes, the cat had tangled the ball of yarn throughout the room, and Al couldn't help but smile. "You, silly cat. Are you trying to lock me up here?" She sighed and untangled the strands, rolling the end of the yarn around her fingers. Following the path, she ended up standing before an abstract statue on the bookshelf. Hidden behind it, she noticed a CD, wrapped in plastic, with the letters A-B printed on it. "Hmmmm, are you giving me clues to get out of this maze?" She put the CD in the overcoat pocket and grabbed Miguel's laptop. Later, all the clues collected would be analyzed. Cheshire purred with a final caress from Al. If she had been less confused, she might've said he winked.

"Let's go to the *Paseo de la Castellana*", she informed the taxi driver. Only after situating her luggage in the trunk and sitting in the back seat was Al able to relax. That was when she realized how angry she was because of the uncertainty of not knowing if Miguel was involved in all this with Beta, but would soon find out.

"What was on that CD?" It wasn't Al's nature to take something without authorization, but they messed with her first. "That didn't justify my error," is what she would say to Julia as a mother. She had been extremely contradictory during this trip. Good thing that by this time tomorrow, she would be landing in Brazil, back to the known and routine. She even missed basic tasks like going to the grocery store, waking her daughter up for school, paying the housekeeper, and caring for the garden. The taxi driver claimed they had arrived and charged her for the ride.

Alberta waited in the lobby as the front desk informed Carlos that a thin, almost bald, extremely blonde woman full of suitcases and bags wanted to go up to his room. If she had a choice, that would be the last place she'd return to in Madrid. But there wasn't any. She was back at the scene of the whiskey dick, and bet there wouldn't be a pull-out bed available for her.

"Since you're asking, I think it was naive of you to stay in Angelo's, or Miguel's, or whoever's apartment without even knowing the guy personally."

"Carlos, the worst part is that it feels like I already knew him."

"As Beta, you mean?"

"It's weird, but it seems like she dictated the book from the start."

"Damn, Al, I didn't think you believed in spiritualism."

"I don't. But I can't find another explanation."

"Okay. So, tell me everything from the beginning."

Alberta was in Carlos' room, sitting in the only spot she found when she came in. Luckily, she grabbed the chair before Carlos could and avoided having to sit on the bed. There wasn't a couch as previously predicted. Just a double bed, and the chair attached to a table that served as a desk. Al shared that she canceled her original flight because she heard Beta in her head, saying that she didn't need to be in Madrid physically. She sent her character instead to collect the information and record it in the book. At first, she stayed at a hotel in *Guarulhos* and then at *Augusta.*

"How many days?" Carlos asked.

Alberta had to think about it.

"If my flight was on Friday night and I only arrived Wednesday morning, it would be five days."

"Half the trip? That's impossible."

"What do you mean by impossible?"

"I called you on Sunday, and you were here. You're telling me I spoke to Beta?"

"No, you didn't. I actually pretended I was here" she confessed, embarrassed.

"Oh, I see…"

"Sorry, Carlos. I thought it was just a little lie. I was tired. Anyway, I got myself into a mess, didn't I?"

"I'm going to ask for half of your advance back." He threatened, smiling.

"I'll give it all back, I promise!"

"Continue."

Al said she researched what exhibitions were happening at the museums, the weather in the city, where the hotel was, and the most covert bars. All using websites, blogs, newspapers, apps, and whatever the internet offered about Madrid. The problem started when she included real characters into the plot. The first was her friend Anita, whom Beta met up with at the *Prado.* They drank, and she asked to be introduced to one of her

Spanish friends. Carlos laughed, anticipating what was coming next. Al wanted to know what he was laughing about.

"You're telling me that Beta chose Angelo?"

"I know. It's absurd. But she wanted some random Miguel, and I thought she chose him based on the Facebook picture that Anita showed her. I didn't describe the picture in the book. It was just the name based on the character's previous history. Without knowing his name is Miguel Angelo, and he used both names."

Al didn't know if Carlos believed in her anymore, yet she persisted, saying her internet stopped working, and the hotel concierge in Spain told her she received flowers from an unknown sender. The hotel reservation she thought she had canceled.

"Your phone bill can prove all of this."

"Good one, Carlos! I hadn't thought of that."

She noticed the situation was grave when her laptop was invaded and Beta rewrote a sexual chapter that Al had written, using spicier details about Miguel and his apartment. On top of that, she posted pictures on her social media that looked like Al with a committed man. Al thought it was best to speak to Beta personally, or whoever was messing with her, with the book, and her reputation. From then on, Carlos had heard of Beta from Miguel at the dinner where they met.

"Maybe Miguel was bluffing."

"Initially, I thought so too. But then he mentioned an intimate detail that Beta and I have in common."

Carlos didn't know how to deal with that new piece of information. Alberta saw the same look he had at dinner on the game day, and was sure he was jealous. She stopped speaking and, once again, felt guilty for something she hadn't done. Ending the conversation, she asked about taking a shower. Carlos agreed, somewhat uninterested. Al locked herself in the bathroom, wanting to learn one of Beta's tricks and evaporate. She turned on the shower, but sat on the toilet, not wanting to go in, while hearing Carlos calling someone. Maybe it was a good idea to break the tension that had built after the "intimate detail" was mentioned.

Hoping Carlos would already be asleep and wanting to be alone, she took centuries in the shower. How had she gotten herself into this mess?

She opened the door fully dressed, and the tiny bit of hair left on her head was wet. It looked like someone was stepping out of a gas chamber with all of the smoke that flooded the room. She considered joking about how she looked, but decided against it. Carlos was in the same position and let her know he had ordered a pizza to accompany the rest of the story. Before she said anything else, he added:

"Are you sure you didn't sleep with this guy, Al?"

It wasn't a good moment to admit he was the very same guy from Morro de SP, so she kept it.

"Fuck, Carlos. Either you believe my story or you don't. You've known me for a thousand years!"

"It's just that nothing makes sense. And the day I saw you guys together, I thought it was weird that you had just met. You were so happy and so close to him."

"Obviously, I was happy! I was euphoric and radiating! I got to see an epic match!"

"True. You are the biggest soccer fanatic I know."

"You think I'm making all this up?"

"I don't know. Maybe some parts. What did Anita say about Beta?"

"She said she thought she had lunch at the *Prado* with me, because of how identical we are, except for the long blond hair. But the woman was freer, sardonic, and seemingly a lot younger than I."

"Yeah, that seems supernatural," Carlos joked, "I wonder if her ghost will appear for me."

Al picked up a pillow from the floor and threw it at Carlos. He promised to think it all through and advised her not to use the laptop she "stole" from Miguel's apartment. They opened Carlos's laptop to check the contents of the CD. Suddenly, they saw a list of 178 documents and videos with thousands of pieces of information about Alberta's life. The first video they clicked on showed Julia with her parents on her sixth birthday, filmed by Carlos. They looked at each other, terrified. Alberta got up to look for some sparkling water in the minibar. He wanted to know if it was best for them to stop looking at that when he saw her crying, a sight he hadn't seen in their twenty years of intense coexistence. The two embraced in a long, timeless moment.

It was late, and they were tired. Carlos promised he would find a culprit or an explanation. Beta and Miguel must be impostors. He would call Anita now to figure out what had happened at the museum. "No, better to do that tomorrow." It was too late, and they would embark together in the morning towards São Paulo. It was best for them to sleep. Everything was too heavy, too tense, and their brains couldn't think anymore. At the same time, they knew they had to continue investigating the CD. Al wanted to call Julia and tell her she loved her. Something she rarely did. They sat at the edge of the bed with their arms around each other. They lay down in an embrace. Carlos stroked Alberta's hair with his eyes closed. The crying ceased. She fell asleep, and he went to take a shower.

The pizza arrived, and Carlos abandoned it on the table without even opening it. He felt a fictional level of sleepiness. At this moment, it seemed like Beta had put them to sleep.

Day Ten

Anyone who thought Beta wrote poorly was extremely wrong. Besides the physical resemblance to her author, she inherited her talent and the cleverness of those born without knowing who their father is.

She spent a long time evaluating whether any part of the book was worth rewriting, but the past was never an issue. Alberta had actually been a good author, but from here on out, she had to get used to playing the role of a character. "Al may have a lot more fun," Beta smiled, cracking her fingers in front of the author's laptop. Now it's time to advance all the clocks.

The morning progressed at the hotel when Alberta opened her eyes. As soon as her eyesight snapped into focus, she saw the red numbers on the clock on the bedside table. When her brain and conscience absorbed the information, she jumped out of bed screaming Carlos' name.

"Fuuuuuck!"

"Hmm. Good morning to you, too, Al…"

"Shit, Carlos, we have an hour until our plane boards!"

He sat on the bed, looking dizzy, and checked the time on his phone. Grabbing the hotel's phone, he immediately called for a taxi. "Good thing we checked out last night", she thought. In the spur of the moment, Alberta dressed right in front of her friend, pretending not to notice that he was watching. They closed their suitcases, threw everything into bags, left a thousand things behind, and looked at each other's crumpled-up faces for the first time that day in the elevator mirror. Al smiled sarcastically, remembering another scene with two different characters. She quickly pushed those thoughts away to focus on a prayer that would open all the city's traffic lights and take all the cars out of their way. Carlos pulled a packet of peanuts from his pocket and offered them to Alberta, "Continental breakfast, madam?"

Poorly situated in the taxi, Al looked at the laptop in her lap and remembered dreaming of Cheshire. She knew she had to do something, but what was it again?

"This bizarre delay has Beta's name written all over it", Al thought while she opened Miguel's laptop, which asked for a password. Al typed Eat Me, Drink Me, and the screen unlocked. From that moment on, she thought she had officially ended up inside Beta's story.

In the dream, Cheshire sat at the top of a tree while telling Alberta to rewrite the chapters before she boarded quickly. That was it. Al started to type before her famous sigh of exhaustion, and Carlos was impressed. He joked about it being a fast food novel, but Alberta didn't have time to rebut, not even with a pleasant "Duhhh." Carlos thought it was best to rush the taxi driver, saying he would pay for any tickets he got for running red lights. It was everything the driver had ever dreamed of hearing. The drive started to get intense, and Al was nauseous. She would finish a paragraph and check the watch, which seemed to move faster than usual. "A trick or desperation?"

They entered the *Barajas* lobby looking insane, and at the desk, they received the news that they had missed their flight to Brazil. Alberta was empty, dizzy, and frustrated. Black spots started taking up her vision, and she fainted on the cold airport floor.

"I cursed myself for letting Al fall onto the floor. My back was turned, and I couldn't cushion her fall. I started to agree with her friends who said she was sick. The Spanish paramedics quickly took care of us and drove us to the *San Carlos* hospital, where I, a less sacred Carlos, am sitting now. Everything happened so quickly that I could barely purchase two more return flights.

Al is getting some tests done, and I am the disordered man sitting at reception, surrounded by suitcases. I remember Alberta was blaming her character for the delay earlier today. And I, the one who is not going crazy, am sure I had set an alarm for the right time last night. Did Alberta mess with it? I adored my friend-sister. More than adored, but it was getting harder to believe Beta existed. Al mentioned Anita, her Spanish friend, Beta and Miguel's Cupid. I opened her purse and searched her phone for Anita's number. Luckily, there was only one, and by the digits in her phone number, I knew she truly lived there.

I called and heard an electronic voice saying the number didn't exist. I tried two more times, but nothing. I went to the most recent calls, and no numbers were there. Not even my phone was that dataless. 'See, Al? You're gonna tell me you made up the one person who could deny your story?' I tried to remember Al's imaginary childhood friend's name, but couldn't think of it.

While she showered yesterday, I called Julia in Brazil to clarify some technology questions. I decided not to say anything to Alberta yet.

A nurse called me to see Al in the room. They recommended that I not agitate the patient too much, but my opportunity to agitate her had already been wasted. I asked if they knew what was happening with her, and the nurse said no.

I entered, and Al thanked me with a smile. 'Don't do that to me anymore', I scolded. Things were not looking good for her. She was riding the story out until the end, even if she was lying about everything. At least the book might turn out to be really good. But I can't touch that subject. 'I wonder if there's any soccer playing on the TV', I said, grabbing the remote control and turning on the news channel. I scroll through the weather channel, Discovery Kids, MTV Spain, and all the other networks without any interest, deciding to go back to the news. 'Turn that off', she says, as if she hates television. I mentioned that TV is a good alternative now because we can't talk about stressful subjects, so we shouldn't discuss what we spoke of before. Al sighs, a sign that she's feeling better.

'And we end today's show with images from the closing events of the International Literature Festival, and with the news that the publishing rights of the controversial book by Brazilian author Alberta Fable were ceded to publisher Miguel Angelo Borges in a highly disputed negotiation.

Miguel: As the translators of her first official book, we got an advantage over the other interested parties.

Reporter: According to her Spanish publisher, Alberta decided to extend her stay in Madrid, and intends to finish writing the last pages of her novel here. She also shared that she had one more typical Spanish event to attend to finalize her book, but didn't want to reveal which one.'

The end credits invaded the screen.

'I couldn't have chosen a more calming channel', I thought as I turned off the TV. That news story convinced me that Miguel was truly a prick. I sent him a message the previous night saying that the biggest publishing house in Madrid had made a better proposal, and that we would announce that as soon as we arrived in Brazil, and the son of a bitch ignored me. I opened my phone to search for the message to show Alberta and found an empty email inbox with no emails sent.

'I hope you get a grip and start believing what I'm saying, Carlos,' Al said, watching me and my stunned face. We both looked at the suitcases and bags piled in the corner of the room and decided to discuss the stressful subject."

Beta laughed and turned the TV off. They were cuddling on the couch of the penthouse apartment of *Plaza de las Cibeles.*

"Miguel, you're a genius!"

"You are, sweetheart. This calls for a toast!" and he went to grab a cava from the fridge.

Cheshire went after him and started peeing on the edge of Miguel's pants, who swore and kicked the cat away, cursing his bad temper. Beta saw the animal walk by, meowing and running towards the living room, and then entered the kitchen.

"Did you know cats only pee on people they don't like? You haven't been a good boy to him, meowww."

"You love a bad boy, don't you?"

"Come, I'll help you take off those wet pants."

"Hmm, don't tell me you're the one who made Cheshire do that?"

"In a way, it was me. Did you forget that you're a character now?"

"That's why I came back to you, beautiful."

"If you do everything I ask in the bedroom, I'll let you write a chapter."

"You promise?"

"Meowww. I promise."

"A chapter full of revenge?"

"Hmm, now that I think about it, that might not be the best idea," Beta said, walking away and playing hard to get.

Miguel grabbed her waist and walked her to the room, closing the door behind them, only to open it up again and kick Cheshire out. The cat wouldn't want to be a part of that anyway. He tried to ignore the moans, but the whole building had to do the same. He missed Al, sweet and neurotic. Very different from the one that was in that room.

Beta had forgotten Al's laptop was turned on in the living room, and the cat was immediately attracted by a small reflection of the sun that formed a dancing ball on the screen. He started to play with the point of light while he stepped on random keys. The cursor on the screen ran at high velocity, swallowing thousands of letters and adding many others.

The room door burst open, and a furious Beta stormed out.

"What the fuck was that, Miguel?"

He appears behind her, disheveled and confused.

"I don't know. I'm sorry, Beta. We just talk about her a lot."

"Calling me Al in bed is fucked up!"

Cheshire smiles with all his teeth and knows it's time to disappear. When he reached his hiding place, he heard Beta scream, “Aaaahhhhhhh. I'm going to kill you and your stupid cat!”

Lucia arrived to visit Al in the hospital, and Carlos left them alone. His phone vibrated, letting him know there was a text.

Julia sent you - knock, knock.

Carlos smiled and texted back.

“Hi, dear.”

“so my mom is in trouble?”

“You don't imagine how much…”

“i found out some things from my friend”

“What?”

“her cell phone is cloned, computer is being monitored, there are advanced automatic file transfer programs, and hacked passwords. these people are good, lol”

“Don't even joke about it, Julia. Is there anything you can do? “

“not by myself. my mom's laptop has a remote access program unlocked for me. first, i need to know which computer i can transfer the information to. I’m going to send instructions to your email. does that work?”

“Go ahead and send it “

“are you still at the hospital?”

"Don't worry, she's already been released. I only found two tickets home available for tomorrow night."

"ok. i just sent it. take care of yourselves."

"Thank you, Ju."

"did you see my dad around there?"

"I did. I gave him a ride to meet up with your mom."

"but nothing came of it, right?"

"Doesn't seem like it."

"why is she so stupid, Ca?"

"She isn't, Ju. Just Complicated."

"talk soon"

Carlos wanted to hug Julia, but had to take care of her mom first. He decided to call Miguel, acting as if he didn't know anything about it, and invite him to a conversation. His phone didn't have any signal. He entered the room and began installing the items Julia had sent. As soon as he finished, the nurse opened the door, announcing another visitor. Miguel had arrived with flowers.

Lucia, who hadn't met Miguel, cautiously introduced herself.

Miguel looked at Al and insanely greeted her:

"*Hola,* Beta!"

Everyone was in complete and utter shock. No one expected that.

"Beta? I think you're in the wrong room," Al scolded.

"You still haven't told them? Maybe I should come back another time…"

"You're shameless, Miguel! If I weren't still a little drugged, I'd tear you apart!"

"I thought we agreed to tell everyone the truth, but it seems you changed your mind," He said, pretending to be upset and lowering the flowers.

"If you two think you're going to make me go crazy, you're very wrong. I will rescind this contract, prove that my signature was faked, and dig your grave. You hear me?"

"Why would you do that, Beta?"

"Stop calling me Beta! You've gone too far. You guys stole my laptop!"

"It's at home. You decided to use mine instead, remember? Come on, come back home with me."

"Miguel, I'm going to kill you!"

Lucia was paralyzed, trying to comprehend the scene before her when Carlos interfered and pulled Miguel out of the room. Miguel continued being dramatic, and Carlos warned him:

"Man, you are risking your reputation as an editor by stealing Al's book!"

"Give me a break, Carlos!"

"All this madness aside, they will find it strange that you have such easy access to the pages. All they'd have to do is track your laptop."

Miguel lowered his eyes, and for a second, Carlos thought he looked confused.

"Let's make a deal. You guys return the book, and I'll try to convince Al to let Beta live," Carlos bluffed.

"So you still believe her, Carlos? You're pathetic!" Miguel yelled, turning his back and disappearing down the hallway.

It was time to see if Julia's tips truly worked. Carlos returned to the room, saying he had gotten rid of the problem, softening the tension Miguel left behind. Lucia still looked at her friend with sadness, trying to diagnose some sort of new or rare syndrome. Carlos told Alberta that her daughter was saving her story.

"And she's saving it on the laptop of your favorite editor: me!"

Carlos was truly a master at breaking the ice. Al was getting ready to go home and found the key to Miguel's apartment in her coat pocket. She left so quickly that she forgot to give it back. She then entrusted it to Lucia.

"If you're still confused, it's time to know who Beta is."

Beta continued to remove the chip from her phone and put it back in. She couldn't call Miguel or anyone else. "Shit, shit, shit!" She looked at Cheshire from afar with assassin-like instincts. She figured Miguel's trip to the hospital would cause a commotion, but she didn't think technology would cheat her now. The device was locked, and she felt Alberta could be behind this. Not Al personally, because "she can barely download music from the internet, poor thing."

The laptop wallpaper disappeared, and Beta ran to save what was left of the story after the stupid cat's intervention. Too late. Someone with remote access had been deleting all the archives for some time, without leaving a trace. A notice that the computer had been formatted invaded the screen at the exact moment that Beta heard the key entering the door of the apartment. She assumed it was Miguel, but the keys fell on the floor, and a female voice swore outside. She panicked and ran to hide.

Lucia entered the apartment and saw the open laptop from afar. She loudly asked if anyone was home. She repeated the question and, without hearing a response, closed the door behind her. "Al did say this place was incredible. She's not dumb. Or they aren't."

Cheshire brushed up against her legs, and Lucia picked him up.

"Hmm, you do look like Alice's smiling cat. Maybe Al isn't that crazy."

Lucia was drawn to the incredible windows, which offered a view of the square from above. Cheshire jumped from her lap to the shelf. Lucia was startled and laughed, impressed by Miguel's library. Everything was in alphabetical order, revealing what a methodical proprietor he was, like her. The cat's tail shook above a row of about ten books on psychology and psychiatry, all out of order. Lucia found a Manual on Schizophrenia and pulled it out of its place. The book was packed with notes in illegible handwriting. She noticed a word repeated throughout the book. "Did it say Attention? No. Alert, maybe…?" She put the book back. She didn't find Beta, just a man very interested in psychological disorders. She had dismissed this hypothesis from the start, as she thought trauma would generally be the cause of Alberta's dual personality. From what Lucia knew about Al, her childhood didn't have any significant traumatic events.

She looked for the cat and found him sharing the bedside table with the laptop. It was time to say goodbye to him. She didn't find who she was looking for, and it wasn't her nature to search other people's apartments. She left the key on the table, petted the cat, and unintentionally looked at the laptop. She smiled as someone who had found treasure.

The <blink> on the screen explained everything for her.

Alberta and Carlos were having dinner at a modern restaurant called *Tomate*, near the hotel where they had gone back to stay. This time, they chose a room with two beds.

The environment was intimate, but Al decided to press her internal fuck-it button. A corner table lit by candles and a cold cava to savor her release, her book, and a decent ending to that weird story. Al was proud of Julia, who showed herself to be a little bit more caring with her mother. Maybe she just missed her. She couldn't stop thanking Carlos, but wanted to know if he was now more comfortable with all the absurdity.

"I think I believe you. But only because it's you."

"Hahahahaha. My Spanish version hasn't been too convincing, huh?"

"I could have asked Lucia today if Anita actually exists."

"And why wouldn't she exist, Carlos?"

"I tried calling her, and the number didn't exist."

"Really? From my phone?"

"Yes, from the hospital. Supposing I believed in you, I could think that Beta altered the story and got rid of the character, or your friend changed her number, lost her phone, etc."

"Good, Carlos. You know me so well that you already know my explanations."

"And I think I should believe in you and this Beta. Because, on the contrary, I need to admit that you are both characters, and if I thought that, it would mean thinking…" Carlos decided not to continue.

"What?"

"Never mind, Al."

"Thinking that I slept with Miguel in his apartment and in Toledo, right? Carlos, if I really wanted to get with a married man, I would've been a little bit more discreet. The truth is, both of them studied my life and found the exact way to drive me insane. Or Miguel made it all up because I still haven't seen Beta."

"That's true. Maybe she's not as similar to you as Miguel and Anita want to make you believe. Well, to end this story once and for all, I've got you the interview you wanted tomorrow morning."

"On the morning show? Ugh!"

"I know. I figured it would be the last thing you would do, but some things need clarification. Think about what you'll say without getting into trouble, okay?"

"Okay, okay. Ah, I received a message from Miguel."

"Hmm… And?"

"It seems he came to his senses when he saw that we didn't fall for his game of saying that Beta and I are the same person."

"He must be bipolar."

"He also shared where he would be with Beta tomorrow and invited us to go with them. Guess where?"

"To a flamenco show?"

"Much worse. The morning show is going to be nothing compared to this."

Al showed Carlos her iPhone screen with the invite, and he lifted his eyebrows as he almost choked. They couldn't deny that Beta was creative. It would truly be a dramatic ending to their plot. They toasted and changed the subject once and for all. It seemed like the book was no longer in danger of getting away, or for the omniscient narrator to knock the previous author out in the airport lobby. Time to relax and enjoy. Alberta was so excited that she ordered her dish using her terrible Spanish: *Creme de Cangrejos*. Carlos and the waiter held back their laughs, and two minutes later, the latter returned from the kitchen, apologizing that they didn't have what she wanted to eat. Al understood, and he indicated another cream on the menu that might be appetizing to her. A soap named *Creme de Cangrejos* (!). Carlos couldn't hold back his laughter. Al was truly incomprehensible in that language. She sighed and said that she would accept that. She was in a good mood, but decided to hold back on using her Spanish.

Carlos mentioned that João's concerts in Germany were a success, trying to analyze her reaction. But there was none. They went through Julia's Facebook, leaving silly comments that she would soon delete to avoid her friends' embarrassment.

They called Al's mom and received a message from Lucia, saying she found something better than Beta in Miguel's apartment. It was past midnight, and they had drunk two entire bottles. Shaken by a previous experience, they decided to stop there and ask for the bill.

Alberta was happy and extremely conscious. If she decided to have sex with Carlos, she could no longer blame the room's single bed, or Beta stealing her laptop, or that city that was too romantic. Maybe she could blame Madrid. She always thought that people did incoherent things on trips since the experience was unique and far from their typical environment. She always feared that thought process and lacked the craving to visit other places. She read a lot and watched many movies and documentaries with perspectives from interesting people about the most beautiful cities in the world. She never felt like a trip as a tourist could come close to that. It lacked the art of editing, the point of view of a good director, and well-written dialogue.

But the truth was, she was there. And the game had gone into overtime. It was time to score a goal.

Carlos was gentle but not a dork in bed. There was a weird start, but instincts are powerful, and when they're released, they know exactly what to do. Al cursed them for choosing the room with the single beds, and there wasn't enough time to push them together. He kissed her deeply while he fucked her. Everything had a new intensity for her. It was strange to have sex with feelings involved again. She knew she was going to get into trouble. She knew that with her eyes closed, as she was now. But it was good. They let go and came together lightly, feeling each other's every final movement. And consequently, falling asleep like an old couple.

"Good night, Mary Ellen," Carlos whispered in the voice of a *Walton.*

Day Eleven

Al awoke, smiling with glowing skin, and chose an outfit to go to *El Programa de Marta* on *Telecinco*. Carlos was joking around more than usual with a new complicity that was very natural to both. It wasn't love, Al knew that. But it also wasn't just sex. She thought it best to stop trying to define what happened between them, especially this early in the morning.

Carlos knew Marta because he represented the rights of her culinary book in Brazil. "For a female talk show host, she exceeded my expectations," Al evaluated mentally. In the network hallway, the two had the opportunity to chat a bit, and Marta demonstrated an interest in the author's problems and her character. Alberta knew the show was hosted alongside a puppet named Mico, who could do or say more inadequate things than the host.

"People always find a scapegoat for themselves, don't they?" Marta laughed with a thick layer of foundation on her face.

Al also had to do her makeup like a clown to "handle the studio lights," as someone had said. She wanted to know where Beta and Miguel were, but figured they would have an opportunity to meet up that day in person. It might be their last.

Marta called Alberta to the stage after a small introduction to her "case." The writer then discovered she would participate in a segment of the show called Tea Time.

"So you're saying your character gained life and started to mess up yours?"

"It might seem crazy, but that's more or less the story."

"And it seems like that wasn't the initial theme of your book. You announced that it was about the conflict between reality and virtual life in this day and age, is that correct?"

"At first, I just wanted to prove that I could write a book solely traveling through the internet and the millions of technologies we use daily."

"After all, many people have already traveled and posted it online, right?"

"Exactly. But I discovered that the line between these two worlds is very narrow. I enjoy reading fantasy, but I never believed a virtual person could suddenly become real."

"And you think that truly happened?"

"In the beginning, I did and even used a bit of that in the book. But now I believe that I was the victim of virtual piracy. These people steal your passwords, clone your social media accounts, and end up finding out more about you and your life than you would like."

"That's why we're constantly alerted about the dangers of virtual overexposure…"

"Yes, but it's challenging to maintain this information to yourself when you become well-known. I think in Spain, as in Brazil, people avidly like to follow, like, and see other people's lives. And I'm not even a celebrity," Al laughed.

"For the viewers who still haven't heard your story, we need to share that your character went out with a married man and posted pictures on your Facebook as if it were you, appeared at an autograph session in your place, signed contracts without your authorization, stole your laptop, and rewrote chapters in your book."

"And also made it seem like I was crazy. But yes, I think you summed it all up."

"If she really exists and is watching the show now, what would you like to say to her?"

"Well, I would say that she should be careful because I can take my anger out on her by making her only have four fingers like they do in cartoons."

"Wow, even angry, you're too nice."

Beta laughed as she watched that.

"Since you mentioned cartoons, you can make a piano fall on her head, an anvil, or a safe…" Marta suggested.

The audience laughed at the host's suggestion.

"That's true, Marta! Or we can think of something very dramatic…"

"Like what?" Marta instigated.

"I don't know. I could make her get a horrible venereal disease. Better yet, she could get pregnant by the married man. How about triplets?"

"That's better! And tell me, have you met her face to face?"

"Not yet. Mainly because I don't know if she actually exists or if it's some other people playing a technological trick. It's possible that all the contact we've had was forged."

"And what about the theory that you planned all of this and that you and she are the same person?"

"In fiction, anything is possible. But in real life, a good detective would discover that my version of someone pretending to be me is the correct one."

"I would like to thank you, Alberta. Even though we don't know the ending of your story, we will close things out today with what you have told me to be the last sentence of your book: 'Or not.' "

The audience erupted in applause for the host and the interviewee.

"Now we must buy the book to know more, right, everyone?" Marta concluded with a wink to the author.

Alberta looked to Carlos, standing in the wings, proud and relieved. She and her fake Twitter profile had just gained another thousand Spanish followers each.

Beta looked at her hands and knew the four-finger thing was just one of Al's jokes.

She also doubted that she would die squashed by a piano, an anvil, or a safe, or with an illness, or pregnant. Her author had good taste and would kill her in an acceptable way, up close and personal. Characters shouldn't fear death, and yet Beta was sad. She felt they were the same person divided, and that solitude was a common factor in both worlds.

"Miguel no longer acted the same because he had the foolishness that came with being of flesh and blood. Men are only good on paper", Beta thought. In real life, they continuously fought for attention, acting as spoiled children, pushing boundaries. He must already be out looking for another affair. She thought Al wouldn't agree to the meeting that night and was surprised when Carlos confirmed. "Was it a bluff?"

Al had found the path to negate Beta's existence through technology. But she knew her author was curious about what was yet to come. She had made Alberta stay a bit longer in Spain, break her own rules, go after what she wanted, and celebrate her wins with a good fuck. Which took way too long, but happened. Al would say she always expected a little more than most, so that she could enjoy herself. Beta would say that destiny guides those who consent and drags those who resist it. And in Madrid, Beta's last name was Destiny.

The character liked the part where she was the story's author. Miguel was still in love and agreed to stay in the game. Deep down, maybe he wanted to punish Alberta because she would never fall in love with him. He was obsessed with Al, owning so many copies of her book, which were completely highlighted and full of psychological interpretations of the character.

“Everything is ready,” she thought. Unlike Al, Beta didn't have a suitcase to pack or people to miss. She lived briefly, but would mark the pages of a book with intense experiences. As each edition of the book was released, she would multiply. She would live in so many different places and affect all kinds of people.

It’s time. We finally made it to page 165.

If I were the reader now, I, Alberta, would love to skip these pages and go directly to the last one that clarified everything. But I can't spare you from the following scenes, which are essential to the context. I'll take the book back from anyone who refuses to continue from here on out. If you have any morally justifiable motives, I'll even refund you. Welcome to the bullfighting chapter.

In case you haven't noticed, I no longer need quotation marks. I, Alberta, have returned to the first person. This is because I'm writing after living the experiences of this chapter, which I wish had been fictional.

Since I heard about the bullfight, I had almost 24 hours to prepare myself. I decided not to think too much about my opinions on animal cruelty and approach the event as a spectacle. It's one with bad taste, but it's a show nonetheless. I never struggled with doing research for a character and understanding their motivations that explain particular behavior, even the sick ones. My curiosity and desire to finish that book dragged me into the arena.

I went with Carlos that afternoon, and the large crowd that an event like that drew to the *Plaza de las Ventas* impressed me. We were not in the *Feria de San Isidro* season, which brought daily bull fights to the city in July. We discovered through Miguel that the isolated event had highly contested tickets, as they rarely happened in the winter in Madrid. It was cold, and the audience was extremely elegant. We would find Miguel and Beta in an exclusive area inside the stadium since we didn't have to stop at the box office.

I didn't know if I could stomach the *faena* or the *suerte de matar*. The third act of the fight is when the fighter confronts the bull alone, already hurt but still extremely furious, to deliver the final blow with a sword to its back, straight through the beast's heart. I sighed and broke out in a cold sweat. Searching online before going, I learned that if the audience deemed the bull exceptionally brave, courageous, and strong, they could pardon him. "All I had to do was convince the entire audience to root for the bull", I thought naively. Not an easy thing to do…

At the press entrance, where we would be sitting, I was shocked by the number of columnists from prominent Spanish newspapers. They commented that Catalonia prohibited *toreros* after a petition signed by 180,000 people, many from the younger population who condemned the event's cruelty. Beyond that, it was difficult to fight for space within the cheap entertainment sphere, including soccer and video games, which that age group usually preferred. In Spain, the price of the bullfights is equivalent today to that of the operas. I was surprised to learn that the night's show cost roughly $350,000. Even more surprised to see about ten people in the stands holding blood-stained posters, defending animal rights. Would they be able to watch until the end?

I soon noticed the ambiguous and radical feelings that a bullfight aroused. The enthusiasts saw it all as a cultural event, arguing that there were equal risks for both bull and bullfighter. They also mentioned an excerpt from João Cabral de Melo Neto on a website: "A person must live at the extreme of oneself. I see this in bullfighting. A good bullfighter gives the public the impression that he will die." The *matador* is forced to incite the bull to attack him violently, and make the animal pass by almost brushing against his body. According to the Spanish, *exponerse* (expose yourself, risk yourself) is the most appreciated verb in the country.

I was exposed, not willing. We found Miguel alone, saying that Beta had left to purchase some *almohadillas*, small, colorful pillows that the spectators sat on during the fight. Watching the bull piss himself in fear as he was about to die, and seeing him drool blood was too much. There would be eight more of those throughout the night. I cried with a broken heart and felt waves of nausea while dragging my pale self to the closest bathroom to wet my wrists. From there, I could hear the crowd's cheers growing along with the sound of water flowing out of the tap and hitting the sink. Water that wouldn't wash the blood away from me. With my blood pressure low, I staggered to the nearest toilet and sat down. I should have gone to the infirmary, which was packed with people with weak stomachs and excessive animal sympathy. I was going to leave, I decided as I leaned my head on the toilet valve. Nauseous, I felt a hand stroke my hair,

"Open your mouth and swallow some salt."

I obeyed, already surrendered.

"Tsk, tsk, tsk. You and your conflicting morality."

It was her. I didn't need to (and wasn't able to) open my eyes to confirm. If she wanted to poison me, now would be the time to swallow it without protest. But it was just salt.

"Here I am, saving the person who came here to kill me, right?"

"A rhetorical question?" I said in a very low tone, as I slowly recovered.

"All because you learned that the visionary has to die," Beta snorted, imitating me. "You're so predictable, Al…"

"And you're so arrogant, Beta. You do deserve to die."

"*Olé*! Is my little author getting angry? Let's end this already. Although I think it's unfair and quite dangerous for you."

"Why is it dangerous?"

"You could die too."

"Too much consciousness for one character, Beta. I thought you were like bulls who act on instinct without knowing they're dying."

"I may have inherited some of your stupid morality."

We heard shouts of *Torero*! and *Olé!* echoing through the bathroom tiles. I remembered one of the ways to kill a bull, which was called *Al encuentro*. How ironic.

"Don't worry. I've planned a pretty interesting death for you," I lied.

"Like during sex?"

"Less interesting."

The crowd went silent, and suddenly we heard a loud wail. Beta narrated for me.

"At this moment, one of the matadors left the ring."

"Dead?" I wanted to know.

Beta laughed and responded:

"Dead of anger and ready to get his revenge on the bull."

I didn't know what to say. I didn't know if that was actually happening. It was all too absurd and intense at the same time. Was I really having a conversation with a character?

"Have you heard of Portuguese bullfighting, Al?"

"No," I admitted, trying to concentrate on the conversation.

"They don't have the death spectacle at the end. They slaughter the animals outside the arena where no one can see."

"Are you giving me ideas?"

"I guess. It's always good to reevaluate what we think is right. This bull fight, for example. Most people arrive pitying the bull, but once they see the bullfighter standing in front of an enraged animal much bigger than he is, they end up rooting for their kind, practically begging him to sacrifice the animal. Symbolic, right? There, the bullfighters become heroes. Small, young, and with balls big enough to face the fear of death, and the audience's boos."

"Are you comparing me to a bullfighter?"

"You tell me, Al. I'm instinctive. I was born from a part of you that is raw and insane. You used me for my courage from the beginning."

"That's why characters are born. None of them has ever complained."

"Well, then you should have created a less well-rounded character. Less you."

"I did consider rewriting everything."

"There are facts that you can't erase."

"But you also can't make it so public..."

"You've already entered the arena. You need to give the audience something soon. You need to give them the blow right in the heart, or else you'll be booed by thousands of people. The crazy, schizophrenic marketer," Beta's ironic tone lit a hatred in me that I wasn't familiar with. "The only choice you need to make is whether you want to kill me in front of everyone."

She was challenging me. Maybe it was time to put an end to that petulance. If only I had a very sharp sword! In that very instant, Beta staggered, resting her back against a corner of the bathroom, slowly sliding down until she was sitting on the floor. A trail of blood stained the wall behind her, and I muffled the scream I wanted to let out with my hand. She laughed at my reaction, somewhat stunned.

"Where did that blood come from?" I begged to know.

"It's ending."

"It wasn't me, was it?"

"You're erasing the character."

"No! I don't want it to be this way!"

The blood slowly poured out through her nose and mouth. I thought about offering her some toilet paper, but I just stood there, waiting. Part of her body blocked the door, and a red puddle formed around her. I was afraid that I would be accused of murder. I needed to call someone and get her to the infirmary now. My anger turned into an immense fear, which paralyzed me.

She smiled sarcastically with a furious look in her eyes. Once again, the crowd's screams in the arena invaded my ears. I imagined the bullfighter and his *muleta* (what they call the red cape) shaking and goading the animal.

I tried to quickly type a different final chapter for the book on my phone, but I gave up and thought it best to call Carlos. I had no signal, my hands shook, and the device fell into the toilet. But I couldn't leave there alone. I needed to prove that Beta wasn't just a creation in my mind. "I lost the chance to photograph her", I thought. In the same instant, I cursed myself for these stupid thoughts. I should be trying to help the person who's agonizing on the floor. I was cold, vile, and seized my cruelty then and there. The anger from that arena had truly been contagious.

I approached Beta and dirtied myself with her blood. There was nothing I could do. I would no longer be able to pardon her. I didn't want to save her. That needed to be done. Her death represented that I was once again in control and needed to subdue my instincts.

I was crying convulsively when I saw two nurses come in with a stretcher and remove Beta's body. Soon, two janitors came by to clean everything and spray disinfectant. There, all clean. Bring on the next bull. My hands were stained with dry blood, but no one noticed. They looked at me with pride as someone who did what had to be done. They asked me if I wanted help, and I refused, static and crouched in the corner of the bathroom, thinking about how I could disappear from there once and for all. I closed my eyes and counted to ten, only to reopen them and find Carlos and Miguel looking down at me with pity.

I felt my forehead throbbing as I lay in an extremely white infirmary.

"Don't move, Al. It was an ugly cut."

Instinctively, I brought my right hand to the bandage on my forehead. My wrists were bruised, my elbows were scraped, and my pelvis ached when I moved. I wanted to know what had happened.

"You fainted in the bathroom and ended up cutting yourself," Carlos whispered.

My clothes had dried blood stains, and I didn't know if I should explain everything I had experienced. Who would believe me? I sighed, looked at Miguel, and asked about Beta. He gave me a disconcerted smile and told me not to worry about her; she was doing much better than I was.

"Here in the infirmary?" I wanted to know.

"She was the one who warned us about you. Carlos can prove it."

Carlos shook his head like a puppy, telling me to rest and that we'd talk about it later. I obeyed, relieved that I wouldn't have to return to the bull fight and that Beta was alive. But how could she be doing better than me? How many lives did she have?

I was under the impression that they were tricking me and treating me as if I were crazy, like when parents planned a lie so they didn't have to tell their child the truth. There must be so many of those in my story. Everything has already lasted too long. They must have given me some sort of sedative with the anesthetic.

They had made a deal, and later, everything became clear. They gave me the excuse that Beta ran away in search of another author and another story. Without questioning her motives, investigating, or discovering who she really is?!

If they decided to believe my story, I decided I would try to buy into theirs, too. It wasn't the time or place to freak out, come up with more versions, or accuse more people. I sat there reevaluating everything, as Beta had asked.

Day Twelve

I flew back home next to Carlos. He stopped making jokes, and we sat in a friendly silence. He continued to treat me as someone who was sick, insane, or disturbed. Once again, I didn't fight against it. I knew I wasn't crazy, but I couldn't prove it, so it was best to stay quiet. Everything is easier within us. I tried to focus on writing. Since yesterday, I have been officially disconnected and have no desire to open any program that informs me about the world, social media, what people say about my story, comments, or gossip. I wanted to dive into my book, see if I still found myself in there, to redo everything and edit myself, as a final barrier towards what they could know about me.

In 10 hours, I'd go back to the daily routine, to normal life, to the security of the things I knew how to deal with. Spain was intense and crazy, and easily slipped from my memory. I went in search of chaos to return to order. Would the new Alberta fit into her old life? I return having lived through conflicts in the flesh and incorporating extraordinary experiences. I had an unspeakable fear of not being recognized by those I left in Brazil when I met them again. This time, I wasn't just giving life to characters. I had to learn to regain control of myself.

I had roles to return to: mother, daughter, ex-wife, friend, professional. That was one of the reasons why I fought so much against the idea of a long trip. I always have to reconfigure myself, reset my internal system, and clean up what I want to bring back with me or not. Arriving means returning. It feels good to have somewhere to come back to. A destiny that's waiting for you. Knowing that I make a difference in the lives of some people. I had to tire myself out to truly rest. I danced, cheered, drank, and lived everything to the fullest. I disconnected from real life, friends, family, and plans. I would return to my shell, lick my baby, rethink my desires, and find a better balance between rigor and fun.

The cursor was still blinking on my laptop screen, as my Beta awaited the end of her story. I didn't have any more contact with her and missed her in a way. I felt the typical longing that came at the end of the best trips we go on. I opened my first book for inspiration, the copy I grabbed from Miguel's house. On page 35, he had highlighted: "...if I could obey my most basic and primitive instincts, I would divulge my betrayal publicly and laugh about making this plan viable."

I sounded like Beta.

Dealing with the sense of abandonment is difficult.

I sent the book to the publisher, picturing Carlos devouring each word, trying to understand what truly happened during our last few days in Madrid. He would soon find what he was searching for. My denial that Beta and I were the same person and all the implications that realization brought. My best character died within those pages, strangely and fantastically, as our story had been. Carlos would be happy and relieved to recognize that I was the same Alberta as always. He would continue to invest in a relationship with me, even though we both knew it wouldn't amount to anything.

That would come at the right time. Julia told me she decided to live with her father for a while. Difficult news to hear, but I had already expected it. My psychologist friends have long warned me that it is common for teenage children to experiment with living with their father. I hope the statistics say she'll return to me soon. Either way, I needed to learn to live without her for a while. I would lose a daily function and would need to readapt. This was the prelude to her adult life, and it would be a good experience for me, my rational side said.

I helped Julia pack her bags before I even unpacked mine. Which would be adequate in case I wanted to leave once and for all and never return. I hated this 3D reality, which is why I have always been running away to the literary world. I craved disappearing, or becoming my future self, as kids always do. I tried to learn from my daughter to enjoy the now. But my childish side is dull, obedient, and too mature. Julia made me a real person, as only your children can do, but no less alone, especially now.

I took her to João's house and couldn't stay for long. She joked that it would just be some "mom vacation time." He didn't gloat, nor was he able to hide his happiness. I tried to conceal my broken heart, and at least I didn't cry in front of them. I needed to find a distraction. I had the entire house to myself, yet I didn't know if I wanted to stay in the cave.

Either way, I would always have fiction to seek refuge in. Or not.

About the Author

Born in 1976, Jan Bitencourt is a writer, publicist, teacher, and entrepreneur. Her novel "Versão Beta" (Beta Version) was released in Brazil in 2012 and in Germany in 2013, and is now being adapted into a feature film.

Jan loves to work with words: that's her skill, turned into a mission. To listen to words, to curate the best ones, to organize, reshape, write, edit, and publish them in order to connect, engage, inform, persuade, educate, and mobilize people to amplify the powerful messages created.